To Angela,

A Best Seller

Thank you
for your
Support!

Julie Heynes
2021

Jill Hynes' Books

I've Been Running for Miles...and Found Myself

A Best Seller

By

Jill Hynes

Scarlett Letters Publishing, United States of America

Published by Scarlett Letters Publishing
Made in United States of America

2021

Cover credit: Mary Beth Seacott
Back cover photo credit: Suzanne Shannon Vasquenz

ISBN-13: 978-1-7376161-0-8

www.fb.com/officialjillhynes

Printed by Ingram Spark

For The Friend
You broke my heart

Acknowledgments

Thank you, Donna Weiss, for endless hours of edits, laughs and continuous assistance and support. I couldn't have done it without you. Thank you, Mary Beth Seacott, for your beautiful graphic design and proofing as well as the additional assistance with walking me through this process. Again, without you, this would have been an impossible undertaking. Suzanne Shannon Vasquenz (Memories by Suzanne Photography), thank you for fitting me in for headshots in the middle of your busy schedule. Thank you, Lindsay Glennon Gavrity (Hairby_Lg), for your hair and make-up skills and having me "camera ready." Thank you, Erin Bellamy, for lending your face to the story…your story is not over.

To my boys, Joey and Jack, my strength that enables me to go on each day.

Contents

A Best Seller

Chapter One

OMG I want to live in a Hallmark Christmas Movie!!! Okay, I need to snap out of it. Movies are just that, movies...fantasy. They aren't real life. It's time to just start focusing on making my reality more enjoyable so that I'm not spending every day trying to live someone else's life; stop chasing something that doesn't even exist. If you really think about it, who is really that happy? Who has that many colored scarves and coffee shops on every corner, that, of course, always serve hot cocoa? Besides, I have never seen any of these chiseled-looking beautiful men anywhere. Businesses closing, small towns pulling together, eternal hope, and the most predictable ending...a happy one. There are the key players; the best friend, the boss, the character that slips under the radar and the love interest. They all take place in a quaint town, there is always snow, and everyone is beautiful. There is always a meet-cute, foreshadowing, a struggle, and, eventually, the happy ending we have all been waiting for. I love it. I'm going to tell you a little story about a girl...well, let me just get right into it.

With Christmas right around the corner, the café is exceptionally busy. Everyone is either stopping in here for breakfast before they start their shopping, or they are coming in here to regroup and to recharge before they go out for round two. It's so charming and welcoming inside. We have garland hanging from the crown molding with white lights strewn throughout. We have a big wreath on the front door with a big red bow on it and every time the door opens or closes there is the faint sound of a sleigh bell. As soon as you walk in the door you feel warm and toasty and there is the hint of coffee in the air and all of the bakery scents engulf you. I keep promising myself I will go home and write since I haven't been able to grab any time at the café. The problem is, I get home and just want to lie on the couch wrapped in my blanket with my tea and watch my Hallmark Christmas movies. Most days I walk to work, and I love taking in the scenery. I'm always hoping that the walk will also clear my head so that I will be inspired to write. The mornings are peaceful as the sun comes up and shines off the snow that has covered all of my summer memories. I love the winter and I love my town. Everyone is so friendly and close, it's like living with your extended family. This is the part of my day where I feel one with nature and where I plan out my predictable day. I'm usually the first one to show up at the café and open the door. The first hour is the most serene as I take in all that is Christmas with the quiet, the Christmas music I put on when I get there, and the snow falling softly outside the front window.

The door slams and I'm jolted back into reality. "Sydney is sick and threw up all over me. Cole forgot his homework so I had to circle back to get that after I dropped the other two off at school, but not before Joy had a temper tantrum because I am, what was it, oh yeah, stupid and mean for having her because if I didn't have her, she wouldn't have to be going to school right now and missing Paw Patrol. Oh yeah, and apparently, I'm ugly too. THAT I didn't need to hear at 7 a.m. since I cried myself to sleep already thinking that. So, how has your morning been, Brie?"

"Rough morning, Anna?" Oh my gosh, where does she get the energy? I'm exhausted just listening to her, let alone trying to raise a family while owning this café. I don't know how she does it. I can see it wearing on her even though she always has a smile on her face, and she appears to be a constant ball of energy. Luckily, she pulled me out of my daydreaming, although I prefer to call it my motivation. One day I wish that my perfect man would just walk in here, our eyes would meet, there would be no one else in the café, metaphorically speaking of course, and we fall in love and live happily ever after. At least twice a week it happens in one of my movies, why can't it happen to me? Maybe I should just face the facts that it's because it's all fake.

If I didn't know any better, I would think that I was the one trying to talk myself out of loving these movies. Why can't I love them? There must be some element of truth to them, doesn't there? I mean, there are so many movies, they can't all be impossible scenarios. If someone is thinking of these things, it must be because people are doing them. Right? If the movies make us happy, what is the harm? It seems a lot healthier to be happy than to constantly be ragging on someone who loves to watch Hallmark Christmas movies, which is exactly what Reagan does to me every second she gets.

Reagan and I have been best friends our whole lives. We did everything together growing up. One thing in high school we did not envision was still being single at thirty-two years old. We had always talked about what it would be like once we got out of high school and where we thought we would be at twenty-five. By twenty-five I was going to be a famous author with three best sellers already under my belt, a husband by twenty-eight and three kids by thirty-two. As I stand here pouring what feels like my 100th latte of the morning at my local coffee shop, I can't help but question what I did wrong. Ben sits at the same corner table every day when he comes in.

"Good morning, Brie."

"Good morning, Ben, you're late today."

"I know, as I was on my way over, I spotted this poor soul on the side of the road with a flat tire. I gave him a tow into town. At least he can sit in the garage with a warm cup of coffee while he waits."

Ben is one of my favorite customers, he is also our town handyman and all around fix-it guy. Ben reminds me of my dad, and I think that's why I love when he comes in. His presence alone is calming, and he sort of just ties my whole day together by showing up. He always orders the same thing, a coffee with a little bit of cream and one sugar packet which he incidentally never uses in its entirety. He also orders a toasted English muffin with a little bit of butter. There are some differences between my dad and Ben. Ben is tall and thin with short, grey hair, piercing blue eyes and, although he is always friendly and helpful, I can't help but sense an aura of sadness about him. My dad, on the other hand, was always happy and positive; he, too, was a tall man, but his hair was wildly different.

I love my job, but it's not part of the plan; at least it still shouldn't be part of the equation. Working in a quaint coffee shop was okay while I was starting out, but I am way behind schedule at this point. Believe it or not, the tips more than cover my bills. Working here also affords me the freedom to write during the down time in a cozy environment conducive to writing, but it's still not where I thought I would be.

"What's your day like today, Ben?"

"Oh, you know, a little bit of this and a little bit of that. How is that book coming along that you have been working on?"

Pulling up a chair, I looked right in his sweet blue eyes and said, "I'm stuck." With the slightest smile, Ben took a sip of his coffee and put the cup down and looked right in to my green eyes. "You're trying too hard."

"You tell me that every day. What does that mean?"

With that, Reagan came barreling through the door with a bunch of shopping bags and plopped herself down at a nearby table. She was looking a little out of sorts. Ben took another sip of his coffee and as he placed his mug down, he nodded in Reagan's direction and said, "You better go handle that." Picking up my tray from the far side of Ben's table, I stood up and pointed at him and said, "We are revisiting this." He smiled and took a bite of his English muffin.

Reagan is usually extremely perky and always in a good mood. I had no idea what could possibly have caused her to go on a retail therapy expedition. Now I have moved from the corner table by the window to the opposing corner table by the door. Working in a coffee shop as a waitress often feels like I double as a therapist. I sat in the window seat with her packages across from her and said, "Hey, what's up? What's with the face…and the bags? You hate shopping."

"I think my boss is going to bypass me for the promotion he kept implying was mine." Then she cupped her face and planted it down on the table.

I looked at all of her bags that I was now sitting next to, then looked over at her. She picked her head up and was staring me dead in the face with a scowl. Before I could open my mouth, she said, "Don't even say it. I don't want to hear it."

"You were already calling it close with your bills, did you really think this was the best thing to do?"

"Did I not just say, I do not want to hear it? Besides, everything can be returned."

"Can it though? All this wasted time you spent buying it and then to go waste more time returning it? You can't get a refund on life."

"Oh Brie, please… I didn't come here for this. I don't need you getting all philosophical and metaphorical on me. I just need my best friend to tell me that I'm right and that it will be okay and for her to bring me an English Breakfast tea and let me wallow in my own misery for about twenty minutes."

With that, I got up, went behind the counter and grabbed her favorite cup off the shelf, poured the hot water, grabbed her English Breakfast tea bag and put it down in front of her. With a full heel turn, I went back behind the counter and started to feverishly wipe everything down. Ben peered over his cup as I was working, and Reagan watched me in disbelief.

"Is there a problem?"

Slamming my rag down, I marched right back over to her.

"Is there a problem? Is there a problem? Am I allowed to have a problem, or do you just want me to tell you that you're right and get you your tea?"

"Oh my gosh, Brie, you're draining me today more than my boss did. I just don't want to hear any I told you so comments."

"FINE."

"BRIE!!! STOP!!"

"Did you consider for one second that you have spent the last three days coming in here complaining that you're not getting your promotion, and meanwhile there are people starving in this world?"

With an eye roll, and a facepalm, her head met the table again, and Ben just chuckled and finished his muffin. Sometimes I'm a bit much, I get it.

The earliest part of the morning is very busy with our regulars coming in before they go out to work. By the time Ben shows up its usually around 11:30 a.m. and Reagan will come in during her lunch hour and overlap Ben's visit. Their visits put me over that midday hump.

"I'll see you tomorrow, Brie."

"Ben, we are still going to talk."

Throwing his hand over his head he made an exaggerated wave good-bye as the French door closed behind him. With Reagan in a better mood, and returning all her purchases, I consider how I can maybe make them a part of my story I am trying to write. Oh, why is this so hard? This is how my entire work day goes. I will continue to rack my brain for a story as I continue to serve the best vanilla chai lattes on the East coast.

Going into the afternoon, business starts to slow down. Anna runs around here all day when she's not baking and then shoots out to go pick up all her kids from school or daycare, and that's when it's only me again. My midday breather is when I should be trying to sit in the window seat with my chai latte, while watching the snow fall outside and writing. Unfortunately, I usually start restocking, re-wiping counters and tables and reflecting on all of my poor life choices.

5

Chapter Two

Obviously, I'm easily distracted, otherwise I wouldn't still be staring out a window at 4:00 in the afternoon with "Chapter 1" being the only thing written on the page. My new distraction is whatever my foot is banging into under this table. The game is to try and figure out what it is, but all I'm doing is destroying it. My curiosity has gotten the better of me, so I squat down under the table and try to dislodge what has been irking me this whole time. Of course, a shopping bag of Reagan's from her earlier jaunt. The silence is broken by the distant chime of sleigh bells. Who could it be? I'm good for usually about an hour before anyone comes in. Misjudging how far I was squatting under the table, I smashed my head on the way up and saw stars. Slowly, I stood up holding my head. I could barely open my eyes the pain was so bad. When I was able to focus, I saw the most handsome man I had ever seen in my life.

"Are you okay?"

I couldn't even speak. I don't know if it was from the pain or his face.

"Miss, are you okay? Here, sit down over here."

He had me pivot and just sit right back down on the window seat. I had an instant, splitting headache.

Seemingly very nervous he said, "Are you okay? Do you know your name? Why am I asking you that? I don't even know your name, so I won't know if you're lying to me. Can I do something for you? Let me get you some ice, wait right there."

With that, he went behind the counter and was searching for ice and something to put it in. For a city, boy he was quite resourceful and grabbed, thankfully, a clean rag that he filled with ice, and he had me put my head on his red scarf that he had taken off and rolled up into a makeshift pillow and then he placed his pea coat over me as a blanket.

"Thank you."

"Oh thank God…you can speak. My name is Declan. You gave me quite a scare. What were you doing under there?"

"My friend dropped one of her shopping bags in here earlier this morning and I was just picking it up. I heard the bell at the door, and it startled me. Thank you for taking care of me. You can have a seat anywhere and I'll get you a menu."

Laughing, my knight in shining armor said, "You're doing no such thing. I can get it myself."

"Well, I still have to get up to get your order, so there's that."

"You're the only staff?"

Oh, this is how it's going to go down. He wants to know if anyone else is here because he is going to kill me. Although, if he was going to kill me, I'd imagine he wouldn't have just helped me from almost knocking myself unconscious.

"Yes, well, for the rest of the day. I am your server, and your cook…and I guess your bus girl as well. Really, I'm ok. I was more startled, I think, than anything else. So, if I was a betting girl, I'd say a city boy like you is looking for a cup of coffee, the WIFI password and for quick service because you are already late for something. And it's…a best seller"

"Wow. That is a little presumptuous. First of all, what makes you think I want coffee? Or that I'm from the city?"

"Well, I've never seen you before, you're wearing a very expensive suit and shoes that do not bode well with the snow here, and everyone drinks coffee… except me."

"Fine, you win in regard to the city, but I'll have you know, I drink tea."

Hmm…that's interesting! Getting up, I got my footing and walked behind the counter. Taking a perfectly sized white mug off the shelf, I filled it with hot water, placed it on top of a white napkin that I placed on the matching saucer. From the refrigerator, I grabbed the cutest little one serving creamer and placed it next to his cup, and not to be presumptuous, again, I brought out the box of teas for him to choose whichever one he wanted. Walking over to his table I flipped the tea box lid open for him to peruse the selection. Hmm…He chose Earl Grey tea which is my go-to after my vanilla chai latte.

"What brings you to our charming little town?"

"I have some business here. My car is also in the shop, so that has put a little kink in my plan. I was supposed to head out of here on December 23 but the mechanic is saying because of all the snow, he may not get the part in before that."

Well, that sounds like a Christmas gift to me that I didn't even know I wanted. Declan looked like a typical city business man. Tall, perfectly coiffed brunette, navy suit that he wears oh so well and hands so clean and soft looking, they look like they never saw an honest day's work in their life. This is not for me to judge, just serve. But if I was judging, I would give him a ten. He was beautiful, especially when his big blue eyes looked directly into mine.

"Since there seem to be no other customers here, are you able to join me?"

With absolutely no excuse, I said, "Sure." Assuming my position back in my cushy window seat, I tried to fix my hair as I sat across from him. Now I just wanted to die because I saw what I looked like when the day started and I'm sure it hasn't improved with time…and the near concussion. He smiled and said, "I really don't think you can improve on anything."

"I'm sorry, what?"

"Your hair…you don't have to fix it, you look beautiful."

"Yeah, I'm sure. But thank you anyway. You're very kind."

"So, what do you do when you're not trying to kill yourself?"

"I'm a writer."

"A writer, wow, that's very impressive. Have you written anything I may know?"

Obviously, I couldn't tell him the menu he was looking at was my first published work. Stuttering a little and rearranging the sugar bowl and creamer, I said, "No. I'm still working on my first book. It's getting there, though. I'm just hung up on one part. A little bit of writer's block. I just need a little inspiration and then it will pick right back up again."

"I'd imagine a beautiful little town like this must provide a lot of inspiration."

"Yeah, you would think, wouldn't you?"

With that, Reagan came barreling through the door again. This time, she only had her purse and a frantic look on her face. I held up her bag and she shrugged her shoulders with a sigh of relief.

"Brie, you're a lifesaver. I just returned everything else and I had no idea where this was." Turning to Declan she smiled and said, "Hi…You must be new around here."

Interrupting Declan before he could even introduce himself, I stood up and gave Reagan "the look" and said, "This is Declan, he is passing through, just like you." and I shoved the bag at her. "I'll call you when I get home." Taking the hint, she grabbed her bag and said, "Enjoy your stay. Don't let her give you any advice. She thinks she knows everything." She winked at me and headed out again.

Grinning, he said, "Well, she is a lot of energy. No advice huh? You're a therapist too?"

"It goes with the job. However, she is my best friend and she doesn't always like that I'm so opinionated."

"Fair enough…is there a hotel in town that you could recommend? Preferably, one in walking distance."

I had to break the news to him that there is not only a hotel in town, but there is literally only one hotel in town. Unsure of the vacancy I prepared him by letting him know that there is a possibility that he might not get a room. Since this is such a small town, it's still a poppin' town. Living in a place called Christmas Village, at Christmas, makes for a very populated small town. We have a reputation for overdoing the decorations, spirit and beauty of Christmas. Believe it or not, not only do we get tourists, but the relatives of all the townspeople come here to celebrate. If you live here, you don't really want to leave at Christmas. It sort of defeats the purpose of living here.

"If you go out the door and make a right and go about five doors down, you will see Snowflake Lodge. It looks like a store front...well, it is a store front, but that is where the front desk is. I don't want you to get your hopes up, though, because it's pretty close to Christmas and, well, just don't get your hopes up."

"Wow. I hope you don't also have a side job as a motivational speaker, because if you do, you may want to quit."

Smiling, he pushed his chair back and picked up his pea coat and started to put it on. I could feel my heart beating out of my chest and I was hoping he couldn't see it.

"What was the best seller you mentioned earlier?"

Squinting my eyes at him and looking very confused, he followed up with, "When you were incorrectly sizing me up."

"Oh, that was the WIFI password, a best seller, I also assumed you wanted. Sorry, that wasn't one of my finer moments."

"Well, beautiful Brie, you made for a very interesting afternoon. Hopefully our paths will cross again. In the meantime, take care of that bump on your head, and I wouldn't go to sleep. Make sure your husband knows that you took quite a whack to your head."

"Well, look who is being presumptuous now."

"You're right, I apologize. I just couldn't imagine someone as beautiful as you being single."

He smiled, picked up his briefcase and headed towards the door. As if a vacuum sucked the words out of me, I shouted, "Thank you!" as he opened the door.

He turned around and smiled, "My pleasure."

As if all my energy was drained from my soul, I plopped right down in his seat. What was that? All of it, what was it?

Wanting to just take the entire situation in, I just sat staring out the window and smiling. The snow was falling softly, and I could see everyone walking down the street with their shopping bags. I love that it gets dark early, it makes the idea of going home and cuddling up in my blanket on the couch so much more enticing. A few hard blinks to focus my eyes and shake myself out of this dream and I started to stand up.

Grabbing his empty tea cup, I did a double take and looked back at the table. I blinked hard again. He left two $20 bills under his cup. I didn't even give him a bill! Oh my gosh, this is too much. That was a very sweet gesture, but so unnecessary especially since I should at least be buying his tea after he helped me.

Thrilled to be ending my day on a happy note, I put his cup in the back sink and wiped down his table, pushed his chair back in and took a step back and just replayed the afternoon over again in my mind. The sleigh bells chimed as I pulled the door behind me.

As I walked past the window to go home, something caught my eye as I looked at my window seat one last time. Cupping my hands around my eyes and peering through the window, I turned and ran back to the door, unlocked it and ran back to his table. He left his red scarf that he rolled up as a pillow for me. I picked it up and I could smell his cologne. This was better than the tip. Carefully, I tucked it into my tote bag and figured that if he comes back, at least I'll have kept it safe.

The best part of walking home is looking at the Christmas lights up and down all the streets and my lights being on as I approach my house. That is the beauty of putting the lights on a timer! As I turned the bend, I could see my cute little cottage just waiting for me to go in and start a fire.

I no sooner got in the door when my phone started ringing. Of course, it was at the bottom of my tote and I had to start digging through my bag. Tossing things out left and right until I grabbed my phone, and it stops ringing. Three missed calls. Boy, I really must have been distracted on the way home to have missed three phone calls. They are all from Reagan. Gee, I wonder what she is calling about. As if I didn't already know. As soon as I missed the call she called right back, and I picked up. I barely got a hello out…"BRIE!! Who was that fine specimen that you were sitting with at the café?"

"His name is Declan and he said that he was here on business from the city. I was under the table picking up your bag, incidentally, when he came in. The door startled me, and then I whacked my head as I was getting up. He got me ice and sat me down. It was like a dream."

"You're welcome."

"For what?"

"If I hadn't done the shopping you were wagging your finger at me for doing, I never would have had a bag to leave there. And then you never would have injured yourself picking it up which caused your Prince Charming to rescue you! So, you're welcome!"

"If you hadn't left your bag under the table, I could have had a normal conversation with a cute guy without having to look like a fool."

"Listen, all things happen for a reason so stop asking why and just go with it. Well, I am going to let you go. I've gotten all the info I needed and I'm going to let you wallow in your dream world with your movies while I prepare my outfit for tomorrow for my first day in my new position!!"

"You got the promotion?"

"I did. My boss told me after I got back from seeing you at lunch."

"Do I get to say I told you so? Please tell me that I do because that would just be the big red bow on this Christmas present of a day."

"Good night, Brie."

I'm so happy for Reagan. She has been working at that advertising agency for five years and when she took the job, she was over qualified. This was supposed to just be a space-filling period of time for her, but she really loves it there and I can see her taking that place over one day. Only time will tell. When she walks in that door tomorrow, she will be the manager of the entire agency and for her, this has been her dream.

After hanging up with her I prepared my spinach salad with strawberries, goat cheese, tomato and beets. Placing that right down on the coffee table in front of the couch with a glass of shiraz, I happily ran into my room to change into my cozy, movie-watching clothes. Tonight, I had a little pep in my step as I walked myself through my daily routine. The movie that was on tonight could not hold my attention and that is very unusual.

After finishing my salad, I sat back into the couch with my wine in hand and put my feet up on the hassock. My eyes slowly closed, and I could smell Declan's cologne as I felt myself drifting off into a dream. I caught myself before I dropped my glass of wine and as I leaned over to put it on the coffee table, I realized that I had been resting my head on his scarf. In my attempt to find my phone earlier, I must have thrown his scarf out of my tote. Smiling to myself, I put my head back down.

Chapter Three

The sun coming through the window woke me up and I had no idea why I was still on the couch. OMG, I was afraid to even look to see what time it was. 7:00 am!! 7:00 am!! I'm late. I'm supposed to be opening the door right now at the café. Jumping up off the couch I ran into my bedroom and I threw my hair in a messy bun, changed my clothes and brushed my teeth. Just as I took one step out the door I ran back in and grabbed the scarf. I called Anna to let her know that I was running late. Thankfully, she told me not to worry about it and to take my time getting there. Like I said, the first hour is usually just me soaking up the wonderfulness of the café. It only took me twenty minutes to get myself together and walk in the door. Lights, music, deep breath and take it all in. I got the coffee started and heated up the oven for Anna so that at least she has one less thing to worry about when she gets here. Every time I look over at the corner window seat a smile takes over my whole face. It no longer rings of the negativity of Reagan's temporary lunacy from yesterday, but of my sweet-smelling Irish city boy.

Feeling inspired, I grabbed my notebook and curled myself up in the window seat before the rush started. I'm figuring if I get past "Chapter 1" I'm doing well. Tapping my pen against my lip, I contemplated; how should I start this story? It could start out with a city boy coming to a small Christmas town and sweeping the small-town girl off her feet as she works at her go nowhere job and dreams of a better life. However, I'm not in the market for penning an autobiography. At this point the genre would be fantasy because I'm still here, and he left. And just like that, I lost thirty minutes of writing as I sat staring out the window watching everyone go about their morning while I sat here writing nothing. The faint sound of sleigh bells prompted me to close my empty notebook, stand up and look towards the door. It's him.

"Good morning beautiful Brie; how are you feeling this morning? Is your head okay?"

"Yes, thank you. And you didn't have to do that yesterday. That was way too generous for a lunch I should have been buying you! And you only had tea. Can I interest you in some breakfast this morning?"

"Yes, please. I was able to get a room at the Lodge, but I thought I might come over here for my breakfast."

Ushering him towards the table he had yesterday, I told him to have a seat while I went behind the counter to grab him a menu and tea. I kept peering over the counter at him as I nervously prepared his cup with hot water, and this time I took out two Earl Grey tea bags and placed them on the saucer next to his cup. I poured him a fresh creamer and grabbed a menu and walked back over to him. He was all settled with his napkin on his lap when I arrived with his tea.

"Look at this service, I didn't even have to ask for the tea. Thank you, that's very sweet."

"Would you like to hear the specials?"

"No, thank you. I'll let you save your energy for the rest of your customers. I'm a creature of habit, may I get two eggs sunny side up with whole wheat toast and a side of yogurt?"

"Of course."

Heading back behind the counter I continued to speak to him.

"How did you sleep last night? Was the Lodge satisfactory?"

"It was amazing." With that, he picked up his cup with the saucer and walked himself over to the counter opposite from where I was preparing his food. He sat down there and continued, "It really was more than I needed. My requirements really are just cleanliness. The Lodge is immaculate and has such character and is decorated so beautifully for Christmas. It's very cozy. Have you ever had a need to enjoy the Lodge?"

"One time last year when my heat was out, Candace was kind enough to put me up for a night and it was lovely. I especially love the fireplace in the lobby."

"Agreed. It's like being in a ski lodge that you also still feel at home in. Sorry, that is the best way I could think to describe it. It's family-oriented while still feeling romantic."

"We are very fortunate to have such a lovely Lodge that suits so many needs right in the center of town." As I plated his food, I asked him if he wanted to remain at the counter or head back to the window seat. With careful deliberation, he opted for the window seat as he could get a jump start on his work before he headed out. I never got a chance to ask him what he actually does for a living before our conversation was interrupted by the morning rush and I had to start paying attention to other tables.

Anna had come in and headed straight to the kitchen to start baking. Her pumpkin muffins with cream cheese frosting drizzled across the top are my favorites. I try not to indulge too much otherwise I'll have to start writing a diet and lifestyle change book.

Periodically I would check in with Declan to see if he needed anything. Other than refreshing his water and restocking his tea bags, he was pretty much focused completely on work and in need of nothing. Having him sit in the café for the better part of the morning made my morning fly by. I didn't even realize what time it was until I saw Ben walk through the door.

"Good afternoon young man. I'm surprised to see you still here" Ben said as he made his way over to Declan's table. I couldn't hear the rest of their conversation, but I planned on pressing Ben once we had some private time. He never mentioned to me that he had a friend or relative coming to town. He usually tells me almost everything. That would have been so inconsequential, I wonder why he didn't say anything. Ben made his way over to his regular table and I greeted him with his coffee and English muffin. Immediately I grilled him.

"How do you know Declan?"

"I told you yesterday, I was late because I gave someone a tow to the mechanic. I thought he would have been long gone by now. It was just a flat tire. Never expected to walk in and see him sitting here."

"He was your poor soul?"

"He was the one."

"He came in yesterday and we started talking. He seems very nice."

"He does; he was very appreciative for the help yesterday and seemed like a genuine guy."

Hmmm, he does, doesn't he? I looked over at him and he was still feverishly typing away on his computer.

"Do you know what he does for a living? He seems very hard at work over there tapping away on his keyboard."

"I don't. We never actually got around to that. We concentrated more on how he was going to get his car up and running."

"He said that Jerry over at the shop said that they had to wait on a part, so he was maybe going to be stuck here for a couple of days. Apparently, it was more than just a flat tire."

"Well, I hope he brought warm clothes because they are calling for a storm later. Doesn't seem like that shirt and tie is going to help him much when those temperatures drop."

"Can I get you anything else right now before I try to clear some of these tables?"

"No thank you, I'm fine. I'm going to read a little bit of the paper while I'm here."

With Ben taken care of, I started clearing the rest of the tables while Anna was finishing up the last of her baking and starting to clean up.

Boy, did my morning fly by. Figuring by this point, Declan had to be hungry, I stopped over at his table. Sliding a menu in front of his computer screen, I said, "I insist you take a lunch break. We have great paninis and salads."

Declan looked at his watch and said, "Wow, I had no idea I had been sitting here this long." Smiling, he said, "I will take you up on the offer. I'll take a spinach salad with grilled chicken and an iced tea. And while that order is in, I am going to just take a walk across the street and stretch my legs. Is it ok if I leave my stuff here?"

"Of course."

"Great, I'll be right back."

He took his pea coat off the back of the chair and pushed the chair under the table. He put his hand up in the air and waved over at Ben. "Ben, if you're not here when I get back, have a great day, and thank you again."

Nodding his head in Declan's direction, Ben picked his newspaper up and continued reading. "That boy has a lot on his mind."

"Why do you say that?"

"I see it in his eyes."

It wasn't long before Declan came back in brushing the snow off his shoulders and hair.

"Boy, it's a lot colder out than I thought it would be. Can we switch that iced tea to a hot tea?"

"Of course. Coming right up."

He sat back down and pushed his papers and lap top aside and just stared out the window. Ben and I caught each other's eye as I headed to the kitchen to grab Declan's food. As I put the salad down in front of him, he looked around and asked if I could take a break. I guess if I sat for five minutes it should be ok.

"So, tell me about this book of yours."

"Well, there is really nothing to tell. I haven't gotten too deep into it yet."

"What seems to be your main hurdle."

"I can't even get started."

With that, Ben walked by, patted Declan's shoulder and said, "She tries too hard," and walked out the door.

"What does he mean by that?"

"I have no idea."

"I was wondering, would you like to have dinner with me tonight?"

Completely caught off guard, I stammered a bit before saying, "Yes. Yes, of course, I'd love to."

"Great, I'll pick you up at 7:30? Oh, wait… I can't pick you up. I have no car."

"I can pick you up. You're right here. It's not far at all."

"Perfect. Maybe you can make some restaurant suggestions as well. I don't really know this area at all."

"Yes, of course... I'm going to get back to work, but yes, we'll figure it out."

To say I was giddy the rest of the day would be an understatement. I wasn't even paying attention to the Christmas music playing overhead. Instead, I was trapped in my own head. What was I going to wear? What would I do with my hair? Where will we go?

Wait 'til I tell Reagan, she is going to give me the third degree. She worries about me too much. It doesn't matter how many times I tell her that I'm happy and I'm content, she just doesn't buy it. I've tried to tell her that I would rather be alone than with someone who does not add to me or my existence.

She has been dating the same guy, Matt, for the last four years. It's a comfortable situation for her, but I question how happy she is. Matt is a great guy; he is just nothing spectacular. I know that may sound coarse, but I don't mean it the way it sounds. Compared to the way Reagan and I planned out our futures, as every fifteen-year-old girl does, he just didn't seem to fit her pedigree for her "perfect man."

I know perfect does not exist, nor do I strive to find the "perfect man," however, Matt isn't even in her wheelhouse. They seem to hit it off though. She obviously isn't as wild and crazy as she used to be, but I guess that comes with maturity. Maybe I'm just confusing the thought process of a hormone-driven fifteen-year-old versus a thirty-two-year-old adult trying to pay the bills while still trying to climb the corporate ladder and figure out how in all of this you're going to get married and start a family. She certainly seems focused enough and goal driven, unlike me, lately. I still can't figure out where I went wrong.

Declan closed his makeshift work space around 2:00 p.m. and we made arrangements that I would meet him at the Lodge at 7:15 p.m. As the door closed behind him, I realized I never gave him his scarf that I had stuffed in my bag. Now I have to remember to grab it tonight.

I wanted to see if I could find a new dress for tonight since my wardrobe consists of clothing I wore with my ex, Evan. It's not like I can't ever wear it again, but I don't want to tarnish my first date with old clothes—old ex-boyfriend clothes. The corner store, Abigail's Closet, is open until 6:00 p.m. so I will definitely have time to swing by before I head home. I just hope I'll be able to find something to wear all while having an anxiety attack at the same time.

Settling on a form-fitting, red sweater dress, I ran out of Abigail's and headed home. I wanted to make sure I had enough time to shower and style my hair since he has only seen it up on top of my head in a bun. Blasting Christmas music to destress myself, I laid my dress out on my bed and grabbed my knee-high black boots.

My last date with Evan was about six months ago so it's not like I'm a stranger to dating, but I am getting butterflies. Thankfully, I haven't seen him since, and I'm hoping he left town like he planned to, although I'm not usually that lucky. Let me not distract from the perfect evening I'm about to have by thinking of that period of time in my life.

Dress on, boots ready to be stepped into and my strawberry blonde hair wavy and hanging midway down my back, I am ready to put on my red lipstick and head over to the Lodge. I love red at Christmastime, I just hope I didn't overdo it.

As I was driving into town, I realized I had not put any thought into where to go. Maybe he might be able to throw out some food suggestions and then I can figure out where to go from there. We have a couple of restaurants in town and then a handful out of town. All are easily accessible, I just don't know what kind of food he likes. As I pulled up to the Lodge, I was able to get a parking spot right in the front. Candace was at the front desk, and seemed a little surprised to see me when I walked in.

"Hey, sweetie, don't tell me your heat is out again"

"Oh no… thank goodness. Actually, I'm here to meet one of your guests. His name is, Declan," and at that moment I realized, I had no idea what his last name was.

"That's all I know, I'm sorry. He just checked in yesterday." I no sooner said that, and I saw him turn around out of the corner of my eye. He was standing in front of the fireplace right next to the front desk. He was wearing a grey suit, with a lavender shirt and paisley tie.

As Declan started walking towards me, he said, "I thought I'd wait down here for you since it's so cozy."

"Yes, this is beautiful."

"I'm glad you feel that way, because I had an idea. Follow me."

He took my hand and walked me through the doorway behind the desk. I caught a glimpse of Candace grinning as she put her nose back in to the old school reservation book that was on her desk and tried to look busy. We walked in to a small, quaint with a formal twist, romantic, somewhat rustic, dining room that had a river rock fireplace with a roaring fire going, subtle white twinkle lights on the garland that was draped all around the perimeter of the room. There was one table for two right in front of the fireplace with a tasteful bud vase with red and white roses right in the center of the table.

"I hope you don't mind. I took the liberty of reserving the restaurant because you said you didn't get the opportunity to take advantage of the services here. It's so beautiful, I wanted you to experience it."

Oh my gosh, I can't believe he listened to what I said, let alone put something into motion because of it.

"This is really beautiful. Thank you so much, it was very thoughtful."

Pulling my chair out for me he said, "I didn't know if you'd prefer wine or tea."

Laughing, I said, "The red wine will be perfect."

When he sat down across from me, for the first time I was able to just look at his whole face. He really was as pretty as I thought he was. He had a very chiseled face; but dimples that softened his look. His eyes were soulful, and his lips; well, let's just say that it wasn't a punishment to have to be looking right at him all through dinner. "Do you always have such extravagant dinners when you are only in town for two days?"

"Well, I don't think of it as extravagant, more like taking advantage of opportunities that are right in front of me. If you have already been here, you should at least have experienced the full effect of this beautiful Inn. And since you didn't, I'd like to treat you to that. It's the least I can do since you have basically been my personal chef for the last two days and have also allowed me the time to use the café as my office."

Clinking our glasses together, Declan made a toast to new friends, experiences and health. I'll drink to that. This was a perfect opportunity for me to inquire about what it is that Mr. Declan, no last name, does for a living.

He literally witnessed me working but he has never once said a word about his job. Obviously, I have made my assumptions, and we see how that worked out. Before we got in to any deep conversation our waiter had come over to tell us the specials. It felt like this conversation was never going to get underway.

I'm a creature of habit. "I would like the mescaline salad with beets, pears and goat cheese and could we add some grilled chicken to that as well?"

With a sexy little smirk, Declan paused a moment and stared right at me. "That sounds great. I'll have the same."

Hmm, a man that eats salad for dinner…that's something new. Could he truly be a somewhat healthy man?

"I had you pegged for a rare steak and a potato kind of guy."

Laughing he said, "Yeah, you have a very twisted, distinct view of who you think I am."

"I guess I need to work on that."

"Five years ago, for my thirtieth birthday, I decided to make some significant changes in my life. My eating habits were one of them. I gave up red meat and I added exercise into my daily routine, and I feel so much better since I did that. I know my food choices don't appear to be what most might consider 'masculine' if that's even a thing, but I can assure you, I'm quite secure in my choices."

Wow, he really isn't from around here. Unless, of course, I have misconstrued that too. The fireplace was the perfect backdrop for the night. The snow was softly falling, and we had a perfect view from our table. It was so cozy.

"So, what is it that you do for a living?"

Our waiter came over and placed two small dishes between us.

"Please enjoy some warm rosemary bread and some fruit and cheese with your wine."

Passing the dish to me, Declan said, "Rosemary bread is my favorite. It tastes just like Christmas."

"I've never had it."

Looking stunned, Declan said, "How can you live here and not have had Rosemary bread? Especially when it's warm? Take a piece, we will try it together."

I took a piece and he took the plate back and took a piece for himself. "You have to just savor this and then you follow it with the wine."

I took a bite and OMG it tasted just like Christmas. I don't even know what that means but that is the only way to describe it. If Christmas had a taste, this was it. It was warm and cozy, it was delicious, and with the wine it was romantic and sexy. How did I get that from a bite of bread?

So, he knows Christmas snacks, he's good looking and he takes care of himself. I'm intrigued already. The time just flew by and before we knew it, our entrées had arrived. We chatted as if we had known each other forever.

"So, tell me, what is it that has you with such writers block?"

With a defeated, deep cleansing breath, I said, "I have no idea."

"You're distracted."

"I'm really not. I mean, I have my routine and I don't have any real distractions."

"Your routine?"

"Yes, I have the café during the day, I mingle with my customers, and then I head home and get ready for the next day and usually sit and relax and maybe catch up on my Hallmark movies."

"Oh, that routine…so, you don't really do any living?"

Offended, I said, "Excuse me? How is my day not living?"

"Don't take it the wrong way. I mean it's great, you are very responsible and rigid and take care of what you need to take care of but what about the living part of life? Entertainment? Fun? Hobbies?"

"I have fun. I do things. Look, I'm having a wonderful dinner right now with someone who thinks I'm a dud."

"I don't think you're a dud. I think that you are shortchanging yourself and missing out on a lot of life. There is a lot of living to be had and you seem quite content to stay in your bubble and not branch out at all. There is just so much more to life than you are allowing yourself to experience. I would hate to find myself at the end of mine and look back and realize that I missed out on any of what I have already experienced, and I still feel I have so much more I want to do. How are you supposed to write if you're not inspired? You're only going to write about fantasy, wishes and dreams. Wouldn't you want to be able to incorporate experience coupled with authentic emotion to write to your fullest potential?"

Well, damn pretty boy, you really put me in my place. I don't want to admit there may be a shred of truth to any of what he just said. Luckily, our waiter came over and broke up the reality check with our salads.

"How is it that you're so knowledgable and intuitive? You seem to be a bit of a workaholic yourself. Are you really in a position to be casting stones about living life, or not living life for that matter?"

Giving an approving smirk while he finished chewing his salad, he swallowed, took a sip of his wine, and said, "Touché." He has a point, I guess. All I could find myself doing was putting my wine to my lips and taking a sip as I mentally digested everything he just said.

"So, tell me, how are you enjoying your meal? Will you be able to add a positive restaurant review to your already raving review of the accommodations?"

Smiling, and taking it all in with a deep breath, I said, "It is perfect. The food is delicious, the ambiance is Christmas mixed with romance, home and comfort, and, really, what more do you need?"

"That's a very visual assessment."

"I want to thank you for inviting me. Thank you for opening my eyes to a gem that was hiding right under my nose the whole time."

"Thank YOU for being my companion while I pass through town. This trip was to be all work and me being stuck in my own head for a week, but you have made this an unexpected surprise."

"I think the same can be said for you. The anticipation of pulling out my book to start writing and then just falling asleep to the backdrop of a Christmas movie is all the excitement I thought I could handle. So, tell me…"

With that, the waiter appeared with a tray full of the most amazing array of decadent beauty I had ever seen. Chocolate cake, cheesecake, chocolate cheesecake, chocolate covered strawberries and other desserts that would need an explanation. Well, I am thinking, I had a very healthy dinner, so what would a little dessert hurt?

Gesturing towards the tray, Declan said, "What will it be?"

Without hesitation I pointed to the chocolate cake.

"Make that two please."

"Are you a chocolate addict as well? It seems I can have the most adult meal, but when it comes to dessert, I'm an eight-year-old girl."

"I love chocolate. I may have completely changed my diet and outlook about nutrition but when it comes to chocolate, all bets are off."

There is nothing more delectable than that first taste of chocolate hitting your lips. The cake is almost as distracting as Declan's blue eyes. Since my breakup with my ex, I feel like I haven't even thought about getting myself into a new situation.

This is unusual for me, having a non-date dinner with a male who has no ulterior motives. Although, why would this not be a date? It has all the elements of a date. Did I just act like a man and have this whole scenario fly right over my head?

"Getting back to what we were talking about before, what was the last exciting thing you did?"

"I beg your pardon, what makes you think I don't do exciting things?"

Laughing, he said, "Wow…defensive much? I didn't insinuate that you don't do anything exciting, I asked you what it is that you did last. You maybe want to rethink your exciting lifestyle."

"Boy, I can't seem to get myself in check since you walked into the café. I'm not sure if that is who I am or if I am still conditioned to act like this because of Prince Charming. I'm just going to apologize in advance for my reactive responses. I think I'm just beating myself up with this writer's block. If I had to think about it, I'd say the last thing was the weekend trip I took with my ex to a vineyard. It was the first time I ever went to a vineyard and it was nice."

"Well, that is something to start with. Why don't you use that as a back drop for your story?"

Perplexed I said, "What do you mean?"

"Actually, I guess I should ask you, what genre are you interested in? Did you decide that?"

"Well, I think maybe romance, perhaps a 'Hallmark Christmas' type story. I love the simplicity of them coupled with the minimal angst but eventual happy ending. I don't mind what some perceive to be the predictability of them, they just make me happy and I want to create and share a happy story."

"It seems as though you have laid the groundwork. I think you're just putting too much pressure on yourself. You need to give yourself a break. You could be missing the obvious."

Letting his insight marinate for a moment, I took a sip of my wine and as I set it back down, I noticed the faintest hint of lipstick on my glass prompting me to excuse myself. Now seems to be the perfect time to go to the ladies' room and freshen up. Declan stood up as I got up which reminded me that you don't see that much these days.

Looking in the mirror I could see my lipstick needed a retouch but fared well for the most part. It appears I was having a spectacular hair day as well. Those, too, are often few and far between. Taking one last glance as I straightened my dress, I headed back.

Halfway to the table I paused and just took in the whole moment. Declan had his back to me, and he was just gazing out through the French windows which adorned the entire front of the restaurant. I expected him to be using this moment to check text messages, emails or scroll through his social media. What I found instead was a man comfortable enough with himself to enjoy his own company and someone who can appreciate the moment. As I approached, Declan stood up and pulled my chair out.

"This is really a beautiful view. You can see the whole town and the snow falling and with all the Christmas lights scattered throughout makes it so serene. Couple that with a fireplace, great wine and even greater company, you've got yourself an incredible landscape."

It didn't take much for me to forget the fact that we were the only ones sitting in the restaurant. Dinner was winding down and I didn't know what to expect for the rest of the evening. With a soft smile he said, "You ready to get out of here?"

"Sure."

With that he stood up, pulled my chair out and gestured towards the exit. We walked out to the front desk where Candace was flipping through her reservation book with a grin on her face. Declan excused himself and went upstairs to get his coat and I said, "What are you grinning at?" Keeping her eyes peeled on her book and with her grin in place, she said, "Did you have a nice time?"

"I did. He is very sweet. And by the way, your chocolate cake is to die for."

I felt his hand on the small of my back. "Are you ready to go?"

"Yes. Okay Candace, thank you so much and I'll see you tomorrow."

"And I'll see you later," Declan said to her as we made our way to the street.

"May I?" Declan asked as he reached for my hand. We walked hand in hand looking at all of the beautifully decorated window displays. I can't remember the last time I felt this relaxed. If it wasn't for the stark contrast between Declan and my ex, I don't know that I would have realized how wrong he really was for me. It wasn't until Declan had made this night about taking me into consideration did I realize how entirely selfish my ex was. That revelation, of course, made Declan even more appealing.

"So tell me Mr. Declan, what is your last name, and what is it that you do for a living that has you typing so feverishly at the café?" I did it! I got it all out in one fell swoop!

"Well, my last name is Hynds, and I guess you can say I'm in sales. I mean, you can say it. I'm in sales. How is your head, by the way? That was some whack you gave it."

"Yes, thank you for remembering that…not one of my finer moments. Oh my gosh! I forgot your scarf at home. I'm so sorry, I had it right next to my bag to bring with me."

"I guess that means, I have to see you again to get it. That works for me."

He squeezed my hand and we headed back towards the Lodge. This has been the most amazing evening I have ever had. There was nothing over the top, just a respectful, relaxing evening. It was so great, I didn't want it to end. Again, a drastic difference from my dates with Evan. The walk back to the

Lodge seemed much quicker than our walk through the town.

"Well, this is me," I said as we approached my truck.

"Thank you for spending your evening with me. I enjoyed your company and thank you for letting me work a little exercise into our evening so I can walk that cake off. How amazing was that chocolate cake?"

"Oh, I know. Thank you for giving me the opportunity to indulge."

"I know I am only here for a few days but would you maybe like to do this again?"

"I would love to."

"Terrific… May I have your number, although I know I will see you at the café?"

Taking his phone, I typed my number in and handed it back to him. "Don't feel pressure, I know you must have a lot on your mind what with your car, your delay in getting to your destination and work."

Grinning he said, "I can multitask, but thank you for your concern. I will see you in the morning at the café. May I have a hug?"

"Of course."

He wrapped his arms around me and I could smell his cologne on his pea coat. I was hoping that my eyes rolled back to normal by the time we pulled away, otherwise he would be thinking I'm having a seizure and that I need a home attendant and not a date.

"Your hair smells amazing."

OMG There go my eyes again.

Pulling back slowly I said, "Thank you. Your cologne is pretty, um… enticing." OMG Did I just say enticing? Please tell me I didn't say that. Please, please, tell me I stopped at thank you.

He put an eyebrow up and grinned. "I won't forget to wear this cologne tomorrow, I can promise you that."

OMG I did say it out loud. With a big grin on his face he opened my car door and I slipped in to the driver seat. I would have slipped under the truck if I could have. He waited on the sidewalk with his hands in his pockets of his pea coat and watched me drive off until I disappeared into the darkness.

Chapter Four

Well, I think that may have been the best sleep I ever had. Lying in bed, I opened my eyes and just lay there a moment. I wanted to consider if in fact that was a dream or if that actually happened to me. Smiling and rolling my face into the pillow, I screamed. Yep, it happened. The reality check was the subtle scent of his cologne still lingering in my hair. I didn't really know how badly I needed that date until I had it. It was very cathartic. Is that even possible? It's as if that date restored my faith in men again. I wonder what Mr. Wonderful has in mind for his day today. I'd imagine a lot of work since that's what he seems to wrap himself up in from what I can see. Sales…explains the suit. What does he sell? Hmm, he was going to be here for a few days, I wonder what he is looking to sell and to whom.

The blaring music from my alarm clock jolted me up in bed. I can't believe I woke up before the alarm, that is unheard of. With a full stretch and a huge smile on my face, I got out of bed and hopped in the shower. All I did was replay last night in my mind over and over and over again as I lathered up my hair. Oh no; I just washed his scent out. Dammit. My guess is, I'll have to reapply tonight. I'm down an outfit since I only bought one yesterday after work. Maybe I can recycle something in my closet without there being any bad juju from Evan.

Maybe I am giving Evan too much power. He wasn't such a horrible person, he was just selfish and completely self absorbed. Yes, we went on some dates. For the most part the dates consisted of things he wanted to do without any real regard for what I may be interested in.

He felt if we were going out somewhere that might shut me up without considering I may not want to be there. Since I'm a pretty easy going person it didn't really bother me. I got to see and experience things I may never have seen since they were not things that really interested me prior. My motto is, it's not where you go it's who you're with.

The only problem was it started to get to the point that I didn't care much for where I was or who I was with. Honestly, I wasn't even too fond of myself towards the end. I let his wants and needs and interests cloud my creative soul. I let myself get lost in the relationship and lost my voice. That is not who I am. I'm not sure how it even got to that point.

What really bothers me is that I didn't end it. I wasn't happy and yet I didn't end it. Evan ended it because he wanted to pursue a music career, which is fine, but it wasn't something that he ever discussed with me. He was just never able to stay still and this was just him not wanting to put roots down and to fly by the seat of his pants. I have no issue with him chasing his dreams, it just seemed as though this was just another one of his immediate gratification, immature, no responsibility jaunts he was going on.

I should have pulled the trigger. Honestly, if he didn't leave, how long would I have let it go on? How much time in my life would I have lost simply because I went along for the ride without asking to get off at the next stop? I guess I have Evan to thank for being the one to go. Hopefully now he just stays away since I have him out of my system, I'd like to keep it that way. Not that I would consider taking him back, but, unfortunately, sometimes women make stupid decisions regarding musicians and I need to save myself; I need to save my soul.

December 20…three days before Declan's anticipated departure and five days before my favorite day of the year! Anna has noticed the pep in my step at work.

"You have so much extra energy maybe I should take few days off and give you the keys. I could use the break."

Smiling, I said, "Go right ahead. I got this."

"Yeah, I don't think so just before Christmas…but I may do it after the holidays."

With every chime of the door I turned to see if it was Declan. I've missed this excitement that runs through your body and the butterflies in your stomach. It makes you feel alive. Equally as palpable are the feelings of pain each time the door opens and it's either the mailman, a customer or a delivery person.

In all actuality, I think I now hate this feeling. It's too controlling, rather, I feel controlled. After the Evan situation, I don't want to fall again. It just seems like no one can actually be who I need them to be which is why I guess I'm alone. My expectations are too high.

But shouldn't we have a certain level of hope and why must the bar be set so low that we are willing to accept any crumb thrown our way? Why make excuses for them and start sentences with, "Well at least they" or "At least they didn't…" I'm actually tired of it. Being stood up should not be followed up by, "Well at least he called after." The rebut for emotional abuse should not be, "Well at least he didn't hit her." Really, at least that? We need to expect, no, we need to demand more, and we need to accept nothing less than something that feeds our soul.

All of a sudden I smelled something so delicious and was jolted back in to reality when I heard, "Good morning, beautiful Brie."

Oh my gosh, it's him. He showed up. Turning around with a painted grin on my face, I said, "Hey, I think I smelled you before I saw you."

Closing my eyes I spun back around. What is wrong with me? Why do these things just fly right out of my mouth? I tried to get myself together but there was no recovering from that. Just face it, Brie, turn around and deal with your moronic self.

I turned around and he was laughing. "I don't know why I say these things. I swear to God I actually think before I speak but lately, I don't know, I'm an idiot lately."

"You're not an idiot. You're raw and honest. It's quite refreshing. I see you are quite busy today, do you mind if I grab a seat?"

"Of course, please, sit wherever you are comfortable."

He chose the reflective window seat.

"Is today a hot tea day?"

Smiling he said, "Most certainly."

OMG he is beautiful. I grabbed his regular set up and dropped it off to him on my way over to gossip with Anna to tell her to take a look. He was already deep into his work by the time I went over to him. He gave me a quick acknowledging grin but kept working feverishly on whatever it was he was working on. What is he selling at this hour of the day? Hell if I know but whatever he is selling I am buying.

My morning dragged as I kept watching the door, but of course now that he is here, it's flying by. The only reason I realized the time was that I saw Ben sitting with Declan. Declan waved over and asked if I wouldn't mind serving Ben at his table.

"Boy, you two have become quick friends."

"When someone comes to your rescue, you are indebted to them forever. Besides, I find his stories fascinating."

"See that, Brie? someone finds my stories fascinating."

"You know I love your stories, Ben."

I noticed it was the first time in a while that Ben seemed to be, dare I say, almost happy. The good thing about those two getting cozy is that I am relying on some dirt from Ben when all is said and done. Declan has not made mention of another date so I don't know what tonight has to offer if anything. I'm not getting my hopes up, last night was great, he is leaving and I am content. Yeah, that's it.

Reagan came in, with no shopping bags, so I guess she is having a good day. She was all smiles when she rolled up to the counter. "I will have a hot chocolate, no whipped cream. I need to fit in to my new outfit tonight"

"And the whipped cream is going to put you over the edge?"

"Don't annoy me, Brie, I came in happy."

Putting her hot chocolate down in front of her I said, "One naked hot chocolate, so that you can look good naked."

"You should put all the effort you put into your comedy into your book. Maybe you can get rich."

"I'm already rich. I have my friends, my job, my beautiful town and a cozy house that my parents would be thrilled to see decorated for Christmas. What is there to feel poor about?"

Rolling her eyes, "The fact that you are so content that you appear to have no ambition. What are you bringing to the table, Brie? I know you will write a fabulous book if you would just let yourself live a little. I mean if these menus are any indication as to how much you are holding yourself back…"

"Okay, enough. I heard you."

"Listen Brie, I know you don't want to talk about it, and it makes you sad…"

"I said I got it. Okay?"

I got up and walked behind the counter and was now sorry I was even here. "Why are you here again? Just the hot chocolate? Do you need anything else?"

"Wow, well, I actually wanted to invite you to a club tonight. Some of my coworkers were going to take me out for my promotion and I was hoping that you might want to join. That was before though. Now, I'm not so sure."

She grinned and took a sip of her hot chocolate.

Out of the corner of my eye I saw Declan get up from the table with his things. He was walking towards us and I prayed that Reagan would keep her big mouth shut. He saddled up next to her and smiled, "Reagan, right?"

"Yes, City Boy. How are you?"

"I am wonderful and just hoping that I can upgrade that to fantastic," and then he turned to me and said, "Are you still free tonight?"

Putting her cup to her lips and eyebrows up, Reagan subtly nodded her head. Getting her approval, I said, "Yes, of course."

"Great! I don't want to just hijack the date, but would you object to me making the arrangements for tonight and if you would do me the honor of seeing me tomorrow, it will be completely your choice."

"That sounds great. Thank you, I would like that very much."

"I hate to have to ask you this, but can you pick me up? You know, the whole car situation and there seems to be no rentals available. I picked a great week to break down."

"Yes, of course, what time works for you?"

"How about 6:30? And we can do a late dinner if you're up to it."

"Perfect."

"Oh, and dress warm."

Passing a bill across the counter he said, "This is for myself and Ben. Don't give him a bill and keep the change. I'll see you later."

I looked at Reagan and her eyes were bulging out of her head. She was staring at the counter. I looked down and there was a $100 bill. What the hell does this guy sell? I just got an $80 tip from the man who is going to take me out to dinner tonight. Dammit! I forgot to give him his scarf again!

"I swear to God, Brie, you are so lucky you said yes otherwise I was throwing you under the bus."

"Just keep your mouth shut."

"What do you say when he asks you about your family and your life?"

"He's only here for a few days, we are keeping each other company and then he is back to the city."

"For God's sake Brie, the city is ninety minutes away. The outside world isn't far off. You need to get out of this rut…"

"Rut? That's what you think this is? A rut?"

"Brie, I'm so sorry, I didn't meant that. It's just…"

"Maybe you better go."

For the first time she didn't push back. She got up, grabbed her coat and walked towards the door.

"I'm sorry, you know I love you. I just hate seeing you like this."

"I know. Have fun tonight. You deserve it. I'll call you tomorrow and fill you in on my date."

I'm always set with winter clothes, that is never an issue. My outfit of choice tonight was going to be simple. A pair of black leggings with a grey cable knit sweater and the most important thing of all, my white snow boots with a fuzzy interior. As I walked out the door I double-checked my bag for his red scarf. Pulling it out of my bag I gave it a whiff, yep, still smells like him.

The Lodge was lit up beautifully with white lights around the perimeter. Tonight was another optimal weather night with softly falling snow but it was not too cold at all. Nothing a nice warm coat couldn't take care of.

Declan was waiting outside when I pulled up. He had a big grin on his face. As soon as he slipped in the front seat, the truck filled with his cologne. It was just enough. Enough to get my attention, but not enough to asphyxiate me. And yes, it was the same enticing cologne as last night. I can't help but feel that was intentional. He leaned over and kissed me on the cheek and said, "Hello, beautiful Brie."

This time, I said to myself, I am going to keep my mouth shut and not say something stupid. Smiling back I said, "Hi." That should just about take care of it. Anything more and it could be a slippery slope.

"Well, Mr. Plan-It-All, where am I going?"

He guided me about twenty minutes down the road to a local farm. It was beautiful. Even though I have lived here my entire life, I have never been here. It was beautifully decorated for Christmas and there were just lights everywhere.

"What is this?"

"Well, I am still getting to know you but from what I have picked up, I feel you are very much in love with Christmas."

I could feel the tears welling up in my eyes. "I am."

He pulled his glove off and gently wiped the one tear that fell from my eye.

"I'm sorry, I didn't want to make you sad. I overstepped, I should have asked you first."

"Oh no, this is beautiful. I'm actually happy. But like everything else I seem to do since I met you, I'm giving off the wrong message. What is this?"

"Well, I was hoping you would take a sleigh ride with me…but now I'm not so sure I did the right thing."

"Oh no, you did more than the right thing. Thank you."

We walked hand in hand over to the coachman, I think that's what he would be called. The sleigh was adorned with white lights, beautiful blankets and sleigh bells. He held my hand and guided me in. We sat under the layers of red fleece blankets, that surprisingly didn't smell like horse, and sipped hot chocolate WITH whipped cream. This was like something out of a Hallmark movie. A speaker was perfectly hidden in the back of the sleigh so the faint sound of Christmas music played from behind our heads. Not enough to interrupt our conversation but just enough to add the perfect backdrop to our night.

The snow fell softly as we took off into the night. Declan put his arm around me and I leaned my back up against his side, enabling me to be as close to him as I could while still being able to take in the scenery. The air was crisp and you could smell the faint aroma of fireplaces, pine, Christmas…love.

Is this what they mean when they say love is in the air? These past few days have been, dare I say, magical. This whole thing has been like a dream. It's strange going on dates that I know for sure have an expiration date…it's like being an escort of sorts. Am I just keeping him company while he was blowing through town? It certainly is a great conversation starter, however, I didn't want to ruin this moment with the possibility of his potential candor. The entire ride was about forty-five minutes to an hour which seems long, but when you literally feel like you are in a dream, it flies right by. It certainly didn't feel long enough.

He used the time to hold me, make me feel safe and secure and give me a little insight into his life…a little. The ride obviously didn't offer enough time for us to tell each other our life stories nor did the possibility of this being an evening with an escort, warrant it. I did want to know more about him even if it meant I wasn't going to see him again. He was interesting and mysterious all while being open and communicative. Who is this guy?

"Have you made any progress with the book?"

OMG here we go again. I wish I had another answer for him but the truth of the matter was, I have done nothing but think about him since I met him. Literally nothing but work and think about him. There has been no writing and not really much consideration as to what to write ever since I saw him standing in front of me three days ago.

"Oh, I think I am making some headway."

"That's terrific." Yeah, terrific, I can now add lying to my resume in addition to menu writing.

"So tell me, do you have any siblings, Mr. Hynds?"

Half grinning and giving a slight huff, he said, "Umm, not really."

What the hell kind of answer is that? Not really? It's literally a black and white answer, yes, or no, that's it.

"What do you mean not really? How is that a thing?"

"I grew up in foster care. There were other children that I lived with, but I would not call them my siblings. There were also my foster parents' children, three of them, but I don't know about any biological siblings. About twenty other children passed through the doors also."

"Oh, I'm sorry. I had no idea. That must have been really difficult. I didn't mean to bring the mood down, Would you rather not talk about it?"

"Actually, I'd like to talk about it. I have never talked about it before and I think it might be cathartic to discuss."

I was thrilled that he chose me to be the one he opened up to. It could also be because I'm like a virtual stranger and he is leaving in a couple of days never to see me again, so what does it matter?

It turns out, Declan has quite a story. His mom was a single mother and she passed away when he was six years old. His dad never even knew of his existence.

His parents met when his dad was traveling through town…with his band. Seems his mom and I have something in common. Since there was no next of kin, Declan ended up in foster care. He never met his dad and he always longed for that relationship.

Unfortunately, Declan's mom wasn't in his life long enough to share any information about his dad with him. Her stories and any information all died with her. A shoe box-sized container was given to him on his eighteenth birthday from child services. Apparently that was a parting gift to him from social services as he was now invited to leave his foster home.

Having never been adopted by his foster family, The Smiths, it left him feeling unloved and unwanted. It never dawned on him that the only reason he was kept as a foster child and not adopted was because he was simply a paycheck to his foster parents. It had no bearing on how they felt about him, sadly, he was, in the parents' eyes, a business transaction. Even though he had lived with them for twelve years, once he turned eighteen, they recommended he move on, as they were no longer going to be receiving a check for him. His existence no longer served them.

Heartbroken, he packed the few things he had, and got into his car that he had bought with the money he saved from working after school, and got comfortable in his new, mobile home. The checks that the Smiths received that were supposed to go towards clothing Declan and getting him his necessities, were kept by the Smiths and he was given the bare necessities.

Someone else may have grown up to be a bitter person, at the very least not what appears to be a generous, well-adjusted person. Again, I could just be making wild assumptions as I have since he landed here but from what I have been able to witness myself, he turned out okay. I mean, he may have some bodies cut up in a freezer somewhere, but he has been nothing but a gentleman to me. The possibility of overlooking such a tragedy is feasible, he's that outstanding.

Before I knew it, we had been riding around for an hour and he seemed to have spilled his guts to me. The conversation flowed with such ease, as intense as the subject matter was. I can't help but think that his upbringing had what seems like the opposite effect as to what you might expect under the circumstances.

"How did you get that information about your father if your mother passed when you were only six years old? Did your foster parents tell you?"

"Oh no, they were not very, what would you say, compassionate or expressive about anything. They didn't care where I came from nor did they care to share any information they may have had with me. The box that was given to me by social services had some items in that led me to do some detective work. Apparently this was a box that should have been with me all along but it was, as many things are, lost in the system. The box was recovered just prior to my eighteenth birthday."

"That is some story. I can't imagine how you must feel. Have you been able to piece together any of the information in the box that might lead you to your dad?"

"I have gotten some information, but I'm not where I want to be." The sleigh brought us back to the beautiful start of this journey. Declan got out first and put his hand out to escort me down. This was such a magical night I didn't want it to end. Lucky for me, he had some more plans. We walked hand in hand back to my car when it dawned on me.

"Oh my gosh, I can't believe I almost forgot."

I pulled his red scarf out of my bag and wrapped it around his neck. He looked like a model right out of GQ Magazine. Without saying a word he smiled as he took my hand again and we continued to walk to the car.

I can't remember any date I ever had with my ex that was like any of these dates. Maybe I shouldn't compare the dates or the men and concentrate more on what is actually filling me up. Right now, I'm feeling pretty full.

Chapter Five

Today is December 21. It's also the time of the year that you have no clue as to what day of the week it is. The season, coupled with being swept off my feet has me in a fog. Declan will be gone in two days and this is the strangest feeling I have ever had. Getting to know him has been exciting and interesting and I want to know more. I have two days left to learn everything there is to know about him before he hits the road. Hmm, I wonder if I bribe the mechanic if there might somehow be a delay in the delivery of the part they are waiting for. No, I couldn't do that, it would be deceitful and what kind of relationship is built on deceit? Who am I kidding? This isn't, nor will it ever be, a relationship. What am I doing to myself? The only sensible thing to do is to just treat this like a professional relationship between a customer and a server. It's the only way to handle this. Although now we are back to the escort scenario again minus the possibility of indiscriminate sex.

Each day when I get up for work I am ready to take on the day. Ever since Declan rolled into town I am more inclined to embrace the day instead of fighting it. Also, I can't help but feel that this inevitable drop in serotonin may put me over the edge on the twenty-third when he leaves. It's only been three days so I think it's understandable that I am starting to have feelings considering the world seems to embrace "reality" shows of people supposedly falling in love after fourteen days all while simultaneously dating twenty-five other people. I'm giving myself a pass on this one.

I'm feeling like I should share a little more with Declan than I have considering how much he has opened up to me. Maybe I will just try to read the room today during breakfast and see if he is maybe having second thoughts about having opened up in the first place; that would save me any unnecessary sharing on my part. Look at me, assuming he will be in for breakfast today. Shaking off all of my self doubt, anticipation and anxiety, I filled my favorite to-go tea cup with some Earl Grey and started my reflective walk to the cafe.

40

I never noticed all of the beautiful trees lining Orchard Street before this morning. Orchard Street is the secluded side road that leads straight up to my house off Big Tree Lane…the main road running right through town. Like I said, we are all about the ambiance of Christmas and small town living. Ironically enough, there are barely any trees on Big Tree Lane but they can be found on all the roads leading off of it which are tree themed names. Each secluded road leading off the main leads to a country cul-de-sac with about three houses each. The snow can make some of the roads unmanageable in bad storms, but since most things are in walking distance, everything is perfect in Christmas Village. As I was walking down the main road I heard a car crawling behind me then I heard a familiar voice.

"Hey Brie, can I offer you a lift?"

"Hi Ben, what has you out so early this morning?"

"Mrs. Eagan's water heater went and I have to get over there and see how much damage she has. Hop in, and I'll give you a lift. It's a bit too cold today for you to take your walk."

I hopped in Ben's silver Dodge Ram. This is the first time I have ever been in it. I'm used to seeing it parked all over town, especially in front of the café. Looking around as he navigated the snow I could see it was filled with every tool imaginable. On his dash he has a small picture taped to the glass where his odometer was. It was the only "personal" item in the truck; everything else was strictly business.

"Who is that in the picture Ben?"

I saw his eyes fill up a little and it was at that moment that I was sorry I opened my stupid mouth.

"That's a picture of me and my wife, you probably don't remember her since you were just a little girl when she got sick."

"I'm sorry Ben, I didn't mean to make you sad. I bet you wish you kept driving and let me walk to work."

He laughed, "Don't be silly. Death is part of life. You can't have one without the other. I miss her every day but I don't want people to not ask about her because they are afraid it will make me sad. I love an excuse to think about her more than I already do."

"You never had children?"

"No, we didn't. We both wanted children but it was never in the cards for us. It's okay. We made peace with that a long time ago. You're the daughter I never had."

Unable to even look at him as we approached the diner I said, "I know that Ben." I didn't want him to see me cry. I quickly leaned over and gave him a hug, "Thank you for the ride. I'll see you for lunch," and I hopped out.

Ben and my dad were best friends. I see the heartbreak in his eyes when he looks at me. Sometimes I wonder if he would rather not have to look at me and be reminded of what he has lost. My dad and I look exactly alike and I can see when Ben looks at me it's almost as if he is reminiscing in his mind. It's hard to tell if it makes him feel closer to my dad by seeing me or if it's just painful or maybe it's a combination of both.

The lights to the café were on when I got there. Cautiously I peered in the windows before I went to the door. No one is ever here this early besides me. Seemed safe enough so I unlocked the door. "Hello," I yelled in as I looked around.

"Hey, sorry to startle you. I couldn't sleep and just wanted to get an early start. Mark is home today so he is on kid patrol."

I was surprised to see Anna in so early; she looked out of sorts. She has looked out of sorts all week. I took my coat off and hung it in the closet and grabbed her hand and took her over to the window seat. Anna, Reagan and I all grew up together. Anna was the one who became a mom a little ahead of schedule; or right on schedule depending on how you look at it.

Holding her hand and looking right in her exhausted eyes I said, "What's wrong? You have not been yourself all week. I know we haven't hung out as much and it seems like all we do is work all the time but what has you looking like this? And what has you coming in when you actually could be sleeping?"

The flood gates opened. She collapsed in my arms and just bawled her eyes out.

"What's wrong?"

"I have no idea. I'm so tired. I'm physically exhausted and emotionally drained. I'm just so tired."

And she kept crying. I have never seen her like this before. Am I such a terrible friend that this has gotten to this point and the first I am seeing a problem is when she has a breakdown? What is happening right now? I sat there with her and let her just cry. Sometimes that's all it takes to make you start to feel better. It's cleansing.

Once she seemed to get herself together she said, "I think I'm just overtired. Thank you for sitting with me. I'm good now." And then she started to get up.

"Anna!" and I grabbed her hand and pulled her back. She looked right in my eyes.

"Listen, I'm here for you no matter what it is, you know that."

She smiled and said, "I know. I'm just tired. I'll take off early today and go get some rest. I'll set you up for the day and then I'll go home."

She went back in to the kitchen and finished her baking. It typically seems cathartic for her but today she is a mess. I didn't want to press her about it so I'm hoping that it is just that she is tired. It is definitely a viable explanation. She has four kids, she works full time and she chauffeurs the kids everywhere and does homework with them. I'm exhausted just watching her. She and Mark were high school sweethearts and have been together since senior year, until a year ago. They never married but have been trying to coparent for the last year. I think it is finally just getting to her.

Not wanting to push her past her comfort point, I let her go back to work but kept checking in with her. There is nothing worse than letting your guard down then having someone up your tail all day policing your every emotion. I put the Christmas music on to try to soften the mood or at the very least offer a distraction.

To offer an additional distraction I shared with her the fact that I went out on two dates with the mystery man she has noticed in here for the last couple of days. That definitely seemed like a welcomed distraction to her.

"Is he that handsome city boy I have seen in here the last couple of days that has you falling all over yourself?"

"That would be the one. I think one of his most appealing qualities is that he is not Evan. Hey Anna, do you think you would ever get married?"

Taking a long reflective pause she said, "I don't know. That's a good question. I mean, at this point why would I really? I already have four children, I have my own business and my own place. When people get married isn't it usually because they fall in love and want to start a family and grow together and then later split everything up down to the salt and pepper shakers? At this point I feel like if I got married I would basically be choosing someone who would down the road try to take my livelihood and home from me."

Well, I never quite thought of it like that. Of course, she could get a pre-nup, but, really, like she said, what's the point? Having never been married or in a relationship longer than eighteen months, and being childless, I can't identify with what she is saying. It just goes to show you how everyone's experiences have you coming at things with a different perspective. She doesn't strike me as bitter, just educated. She certainly seems to have her head on straight. Maybe I should pay more attention to what she is doing and be asking more advice from her!

In the meantime, I'm preparing my work day as much as I can so that I can afford myself some free time when Declan rolls up...hopefully. Double-check the stock of tea bags and creamer, make sure I have an assortment of desserts—just in case—and have his cup cleaned and ready to go.

My morning consisted of my regulars still coming in from their Christmas shopping and the café was filled with all the mixed conversations of what gifts they couldn't find or what they were planning for dinner and what plans they had for the holiday. A lot of the talk revolved around tonight's Christmas concert that was going to take place in the old Emerson Barn.

Every year the annual Christmas concert is held there because it is the largest venue our town has that can accommodate not only the townsfolk, but all the guests that come for Christmas. The Emerson family donated their barn to the town to use as they saw fit. The only stipulation was that it must be used for public enjoyment and could not be knocked down to be used for anything commercial or that would take away from the integrity of the town. Now, one might think, why would that even need to be stipulated as this town is obviously one that embraces its small town values and honors its past and the integrity of what this town represents?

The Emersons were smart enough to know that money talks and to make sure that no one could ever open that door to the city businessmen that when given an inch would take a yard, the barn was secured to the town almost as a historical landmark protecting it from any swindlers.

The barn is beautifully decorated with more lights than you could possibly envision. No other lighting is needed in the barn when all of the Christmas lights are on. There are two huge Christmas trees on either side of the entrance to the barn almost looking like two pillars. There is so much property surrounding The Emerson that there are horse-drawn sleigh rides offered as well as an area designated for snowmen to be built in addition to a generously sized stand that serves complimentary hot cider, cocoa, tea and coffee. Everyone mingles outside taking romantic walks, chasing their kids, having snowball fights or just admiring the beauty of all of the decorations until it's time for the main event.

Everyone knows the show starts at 8:00 p.m., but for the newbies, all of the lights all over the property blink just like before the curtain goes up on Broadway—at least that's what I've heard. I have never been out of Christmas Village, but that conversation is for a different time. As everyone makes their way to the barn most people will grab a hot drink to bring in to sip for the show.

With all of my daydreaming about tonight's event, I managed once again to lose track of time. This is becoming a daily occurrence for me. I was wiping down the window seat when I closed my eyes and took in the scent. Why don't I hear the sleigh bells on the door, though?

I turned around and there he was, holding the door opened for two older women as they made their way outside. He followed them out and held their arms as he escorted them to their car so as not to slip on the ice. I watched as he opened their car door and helped them in their little blue Mazda and closed the doors behind them. Not only is he adorable, so are they.

Flo and Ruth are sisters that come in twice a week and have breakfast together unless they are doing their Christmas shopping; then they come in for lunch instead. Today they decided on breakfast because shopping and going to the concert would be too much to do in one day. Trying to shake off this visual, I ran to the door to open it for him. He greeted me with his beautiful smile and his perfect white teeth. "Good morning, beautiful Brie, this is some over the top service you offer here at the café."

"I figured it was the least I could do for you since you just helped Flo and Ruth out to their car."

"How cute are they?"

"I know. They are sisters and ever since their husbands passed they spend all of their time together. It's really quite sweet actually."

Escorting him over to the recently cleaned off window seat, I offered him a menu. Today he accepted the menu and actually asked for a moment.

He spent a few moments perusing the menu before finally asking me what I recommended. Personally, I like everything on the menu so he was in luck with whatever he chose.

"Are we still shooting for healthy?"

"I'd like to try."

"You seem to be a creature of habit and get the same thing every day. If you're looking for something different from your norm, but not too crazy, why don't you try the oatmeal and add some fruit on it. We have strawberries, blueberries, bananas. It will keep you warm and it's healthy."

"I like the way you thought that all through. I'll take that and I'll take your suggestion of a banana on it as well."

Declan sat at the window seat table but facing the window. I'd imagine he wants the view. His choice of seating enables me to see a little of what is on his computer screen for the first time. For someone in sales I would have expected to see more of a spread sheet or forms on his screen but it just seemed like he was typing some kind of letter. It could be that I don't know anything about sales and what is involved in the administrative aspect of it. Today was the first day he was dressed a little more casual than I am used to seeing him. He had on a pair of jeans and a baby blue hoodie, his pea coat and his red scarf.

As I placed his tea down in front of him I said, "Slumming it today?"

Squinting he said, "I'm confused, what do you mean?"

"I have never seen you in anything other than a shirt and tie at all times not to mention, expensive shoes. Today you have on jeans, which I never even considered that you owned and a baby blue hoodie that makes your eyes even more amazing than I thought they could be."

I closed my eyes again. There I go, just running my mouth with no filter. You would think I could apply that to my writing in some form so that I could make a living based on my apparent lack of impulse control lately.

He was laughing when I opened my eyes. "You just say whatever is on your mind don't you?"

"Well, thankfully not everything that's on my mind. You know what, I'm going to put your order in and I'll be back."

I just needed a few moments to myself. He was still laughing when I left. Anna was peering out over the register and laughing at me. Apparently the effect this guy has on me provides endless entertainment for all that witness it.

"Well, I see now what has you with that extra pep in your step. I miss those feelings. Don't beat yourself up over being authentic. He apparently likes it and it's who you are. Don't ever lose sight of who you are."

She's right, I have been saying stupid things since I literally opened my eyes and saw him standing in front of me. I must be doing something right since he has taken me out twice. Okay, let me shake this off and recover myself armed with oatmeal and banana. I placed it down in front of him and considered just moving on to the next table. He gently clasped my wrist when I placed the shallow, white porcelain bowl down in front of him.

"Thank you."

Oh my gosh, this guy is killing me.

Acting as calm and cool as I could, I mustered the best sexy and secure, "You're welcome" that I could, before I died inside.

He let go of my wrist and placed his napkin on his lap as he skimmed the top of the oatmeal with the silver spoon that accompanied his meal. He had no idea I was holding myself together with every fiber of my being as he just casually continued to eat. I still can't tell if he is fully aware of the effect he has on me and if he is just playing me like a banjo or if he is that oblivious to his superpowers.

Right about now is the time that I would love to be able to run over and grab the phone and start to gossip with my mother…as a woman. That is a privilege I feel robbed of, but I'm fortunate enough to have Reagan and Anna in my life. They are the closest things to sisters and moms I could ask for; but no one can replace your mom. I bought myself some time by clearing enough tables to free up some room for customers to seat themselves while I ran in the back to check on Anna. I found her in the back washing dishes.

"How are we feeling?"

"From the looks of it you're feeling giddy but I am feeling much better. I'm sorry about the meltdown earlier. I think I just needed a good cry."

"I get it. You're going to the concert tonight right?"

"I wouldn't miss it. I have to wrangle my shoe full of kids up but we will be there. Are you going?"

"Yes, I think I am going to invite Declan."

"Look at you girl. Good for you; I'm happy you seem happy."

"I'm going to check on my tables, if you need help back here, let me know."

Good thing I freed up those tables because they are all full now. Apparently Declan was a fan of the recommendation as his empty bowl sat at the end of his table. He was feverishly typing away at his computer so I grabbed his bowl on my way over to clear the table next to him. He didn't even seem to notice that I had taken his bowl away. Boy it's been three days and already he is distracted. That didn't take long.

Luckily, Reagan came in and distracted ME. She came in and gave the dining room a once over and then decided to take a seat at the counter. Since there were a couple of free tables and she chose the counter, I'm assuming she wanted to gossip. Giving a nudge over her left shoulder, she said, "What's up with him?"

"Shhh…Jeez… You realize everyone can hear you?"

Shrugging her shoulders, "I don't care."

"Well, it's not just about you so can you curb the volume especially when you're talking about things that involve me?"

"Fine. What has him so engrossed over there?"

Widening my eyes and pursing my lips I said, "SHHHH. Please shut up! What is your problem today? You say you want me to get out there and live and date and all the other nonsense you profess and then when I do, you sabotage it because you don't care."

"I'm sorry, you're right. What time are you going to the concert tonight? I'm so excited, I can't wait."

"I'm not sure yet but I will be there."

"I know. This is your season."

She is right with that one. I put her order in for her grilled chicken panini with fresh mozzarella , tomato and roasted peppers and her side of balsamic glaze. While that was cooking I dropped her off an iced tea and then went to tend to my other tables. Still with his head buried in the computer, Declan barely noticed me dropping him off another cup of tea.

"Busy today, huh?"

He pushed back in his seat and rubbed his eyes and then just like he was taking the entire moment in, smiled and stared at me.

"Thank you for jolting me back into the moment."

He looked at his watch seemingly baffled and said, "Is it really 11:30?"

"Oh it's really 11:30." And right on schedule Ben came walking through the door. He had his paper under his arm and made his way to his corner table. Everyone seemed like they were in an alternate universe today. Ben walked right past me. What the hell?

"Excuse me a moment, won't you?"

I walked over to Ben's table, hand on hip and he barely even acknowledged my vexation. Gazing over the top of his paper he said, "Good afternoon young lady. You don't appear to be as demure as this morning when I picked you up."

I dropped my hand from my hip, pulled a chair out and sat with Ben.

"Are you okay Ben? I don't mean to overstep but you seem so…I don't know, forlorn."

He managed a smirk and looked back down at his paper and said, "Forlorn? You sound like an author. When are you going to start putting some effort into what you should really be doing and not worrying so much about your old, grumpy customers?"

"You're more than a customer to me and you know it."

Never taking his piercing blue eyes off the paper he said, "I know that, young lady."

"Well, you know I'm going to the concert tonight. I'm assuming you will be there as usual despite given your apparent current state of emotion or lack thereof?"

Gazing over his paper he grinned, "I'll be there. Now you go on and tend to city boy over there. He seems to be a bit smitten with you. Will he be attending the concert?"

I stood up, grinned and said, "I'll get your coffee and English muffin. It's a cold one out there today, have we reached that time of the season yet where you incorporate your additional snack?"

Intrigued, he put his paper down completely and smiled. "Yes, that would hit the spot." Finally it looked like he was happy about something. Sad that it is a bowl of oatmeal that is going to be responsible for it, but I'll take the smile nonetheless.

The café was really buzzing about talk of the show tonight. Everyone loves it so much because even though we are an intimate town and see each other all of the time, this is the one event that we all really come together, so many of us actually participate in it. It gives us all a chance to give back, share any hidden talents and participate in community. For Christmas lovers this is the pinnacle of the season.

A final check on Reagan had her scrolling through her photos of her outfit choices for tonight. "What do you think about this one Brie?"

"Oh that's adorable! It looks super warm too, which will come in handy if you and Matt decide to go for a sleigh ride."

"You're right. Okay, this outfit it is. Do you know what you're going to wear?"

"I don't. I'll have to scour my closet when I get out of here. We need to keep a check on Anna tonight."

Still scrolling and not looking up from her phone she said, "Why, what's up?"

"I just think maybe we need to pitch in a little more with her and incorporate some more girl time. She needs a break...she needs us."

She looked up, "Of course! You know I'm always up for a girls night and some fun. Maybe we can do a movie night and some hot chocolate and gossip!"

I paused and thought about it and couldn't help by smile. "Yes, that's what we need."

Scooting myself over now to check on Declan I found he had finally taken a break. I sat across from him in the window seat. We sat opposite Ben with about five tables separating us. "Is Ben okay?"

"Yeah, he is just being Ben. Hey listen, I wanted to ask you something."Closing his computer and giving me his undivided attention, he said, "Shoot."

I hesitated because I'm not used to having undivided attention like this. Usually I'm being half listened to as my ex is continuing to do whatever he was doing or I'm preparing to be interrupted because I am being listened to by someone who listens with the intention to respond.

Arranging the silverware onerously in front of me I said, "Well, tonight we have our big Christmas concert at the old Emerson Barn and it's really quite something. I was wondering, well, I was hoping you might like to join me. I know girls aren't supposed to be the ones to ask but you seem to be a progressive thinking man and if you don't ask the answer is always no…"

Cutting me off, Declan laughed and cupped my hands in his hands. "Brie! I would love to go. You really are something else."

Okay, that wasn't so hard. Why did I torture myself so much beforehand? Oh, I know why. I let Evan break me down so much that I am holding on to what is left of my self esteem by a thread. Well, now that he is on board, I will have to figure out an outfit.

Inside the barn is heated but today it is pretty cold and I don't imagine this evening getting any warmer. I gave him the cliff notes as to what to expect tonight in the way of entertainment and activities. Asking him to go had me a little nervous because Evan had me so conditioned and I was anticipating a long sigh, an eye roll and about twenty questions as to why we have to do this every year and it's so boring since we have already done it and blah, blah, blah. You were deflated as soon as you asked the question. I guess I was prepared for Declan to shoot me down so I was just preparing myself for the inevitable disappointment. We decided that I would pick him up at about 6:30 p.m. That gave us more than enough time to hang out before heading over, while still giving us plenty of time to mingle outside before the show.

Chapter Six

The entire Christmas event was really something to see. From all of the lights to all of the people and the music, the smells… it was spectacular. Ben had worked really hard on all of the sets that they use. He is the go-to guy for all of the construction and electric. It's not surprising that he is able to get all of this work done since I think all he does is work. I've really only ever seen him in his work clothes. It's like he has submerged himself in work so that he never has to deal with the real world. He is available for everyone for every little thing they need done and manages to construct sets every year for the show. I just wish there was someone he could share his life with to bring him some true happiness. There has to be more to him than just a tool belt and pick up truck.

Tonight's outfit was simple…jeans and a grey cable knit sweater. I, of course, had my white fuzzy boots and my white snorkel jacket with faux fur trim. Figuring it was best to just leave my truck at the Lodge, I found a parking spot in the lot and went in to the lobby to meet Declan.

Candace was getting ready to head over to the show herself when I walked in. She rang Declan's room for me before she headed out. Giving me a motherly wink and smile, she ran out the door.

I was mesmerized staring into the grand fireplace. He wasn't kidding, this lobby and fireplace was something to behold. Out of the corner of my eye I could see him coming down the stairs. He was dressed casually as well. A pair of jeans and a baby blue sweater.

My goodness, do his eyes pop when he wears blue. He certainly knows how to accessorize to accentuate the positive. Declan was carrying his coat and he had his red scarf around his neck. Since I gave us more than enough time before we had to head over to the show, he suggested we sit on the inviting grey tufted couch that was facing the fireplace and chat before we left. There was a wing chair on either side of the fireplace making it even cozier.

"Would you like a glass of wine and then we can head over after that."

"That sounds great. Are you sure you don't mind going?"

"Mind? I'm looking forward to it."

Wow, I'm not used to those kind of reactions. He headed into the restaurant and procured us two glasses of Pinot Noir. He made his way back over to the couch and sat right next to me.

We toasted to "new friends…special friends." Friends, love it. Insert sarcasm. I'll take it; I mean it has only been three days. Sure, I'll be your friend.

OMG he smells amazing. I will do my best to keep that information to myself ,but we all know I have hit some rough patches in the past with the ability to keep my stupid comments in my mouth.

"So, any word on your car?"

"Ah…my car…No, well, yes, there is word and the word is that the part has still not arrived yet. The short story is, you're stuck with me for a few more days."

That works for me. Although, I'm feeling like the longer this goes on the harder it's going to be when he does have to leave.

"Well, I wouldn't consider it exactly torture. I've had a lovely few days."

"Well, I'm glad to hear that."

He's glad to hear that; well that's encouraging.

"I'd imagine with all the work you have been doing you haven't had much time to do any more of your detective work surrounding your dad, or your mom for that matter. I mean, I know you don't know who your dad is and never met him, but what do you really know about your mother? You were just a baby, you can't remember much."

"You're right. I really don't remember much. I remember she used to sing to me all the time. Being in her arms always made me feel safe and then her singing would completely relax me. Maybe I could use another set of eyes on the items in the box. I have wracked my brain for years trying to trace things and put clues together. I'm not sure if I'll ever get the info or the closure I long for but if you wouldn't mind, would you like to look through the items and maybe you can shed some light?"

"I would be honored. I'm touched that you would include me in such a personal journey."

"Well, something tells me you're okay," and he laughed.

"Okay? Just okay? You're going to tell me you know others that can put their foot in their mouth better than me? Or draw inappropriate conclusions better than me? I'm hurt."

We both laughed and then his eyes followed his glass down on to the table behind the couch. With not much effort he turned his eyes to mine and leaned in and kissed me ever so softly. Barely taking his lips off of mine, he whispered, "I'm sorry I didn't ask first. I have wanted to do that from the moment I saw you stand up from hitting your head."

Feeling the only appropriate response to his concern would be for me to ignore what he said and just lean in to him and gently kiss him back…so I did.

"Seems we both wanted the same thing, from the same moment. The difference being I thought I was dreaming when I opened my eyes and saw you."

He put his hand up in through my hair before gently letting it barely settle on the side of my neck. It was at that moment that I knew I was a goner. Basically weak and overcome with the need to just succumb to whatever this moment had to offer, my body started to go limp as his tongue gently outlined my lips. As my body grew weaker his now embrace grew stronger. Completely under his control our bodies conformed to each other as if they finally met their other half.

Knowing this was a connection that could not be denied, we kissed a few more minutes. I don't know who pulled away first, but the tension was palpable. Declan stood up and walked over to the fireplace. I sat there staring at him not knowing what he was processing at this moment. He cupped his face in his hands while he paced a couple of times back and forth in front of that mesmerizing blaze. If I was a betting woman I would say that was the behavior of a man who got what he wanted and wasn't prepared for the outcome. With my head resting in my hand and my elbow on the back of the couch I sat in silence as I watched him struggle. I offered no support, I questioned nothing,

I merely sat back and watched a man beat himself up for a reason I had yet to find out. Turning behind me I picked my glass of wine up that was sitting next to his; I took a sip as I stood up and walked towards him.

It was purely instinct and what felt like a call from his body to mine to walk right over to him. We no longer needed words to communicate. A switch had been flipped the moment our lips met. The daunting look that had previously taken over his chiseled face had now turned to an all knowing, confident message that he was giving in to whatever was happening.

Staring in each other's eyes he took my glass from my hand and put it on the mantle. Never having taken his eyes off mine, he used his now empty left hand to gently caress my cheek causing my eyes to close and tilt my head right into his other hand. He used his tender grip to guide my head from side to side as I could feel the heat from his mouth before his lips and tongue touched my neck. I barely had my hands resting on his chest as I felt his hands outline my body as his tongue owned me.

The idea of any interruption at this point never crossed our minds as if felt like we were the only two people in the world. I felt his warm hands on my bare skin while we embraced. He gentled tickled my back as we slowly swayed as if our bodies were one while we kissed.

Pulling back just enough from his mouth to whisper, "We need to head over to the show very soon." He sighed but not an Evan sigh. This was not a sigh of disappointment but a sigh of excitement and an indication that this would be revisited and that whatever was putting this off was part of the journey. He took my wine off the mantle and handed it to me and held my other hand with his as we walked back over to the couch.

We sat facing each other, but now there was an energy that was not present before. It was almost as if we now moved as one; we were completely immersed in each other. He stared at his hand as he pushed my hair back behind my ear. His fingers brushed across the side of my neck causing my eyes to close again. He leaned over and kissed me and sat even closer. My whole body took on a life of its own. It no longer moved and responded as if I was in charge, it was now just responding to Declan's body…and I let it. He took his scarf off and put it around my neck and pulled me closer to his mouth. With one last kiss it was time to start to walk over to the barn.

Putting his scarf back on, he stood up and put his hand out for mine to help me up. We put our coats on and putting his arm around my waist we walked towards the front door. To say the evening was starting out magical would be an understatement.

From behind me, he pushed the door open so I could go out. He took my hand in his as he took a deep cleansing breath and said, "So which direction are we going?" I'm not used to being with anyone who literally wanted to please me and at least made it seem like he took an interest in anything I was interested in. We slowly walked hand in hand as we window shopped again. If this was Evan he would be complaining that we already did this the other day and why can't we just go straight to the barn.

Declan took in each window as if it was the first time he was seeing them. Instead of looking at the displays I found myself watching him looking at the displays. He was a thirty-five-year-old man with the unabashed curiosity of a six-year-old boy. He looked at everything in the window with the wide eyed wonder of that small boy who never got to experience something so simple and yet so special. I found myself looking at him through new eyes. As sexy and gentlemanly as he was, there was something about him that I wanted to comfort and protect from the mean world.

The music store always has my favorite display. This year it was very nostalgic. There is always at least one instrument in the display and the theme incorporates the instrument. This year there was a Santa Claus looking in what is supposed to be a mirror. The image in the mirror, which is an additional display facing Santa, was a younger version of Santa. They were both holding the exact same Gibson Les Paul by the neck and the body of it was touching the floor. Both Santas were bent over a little as if they were each peering into either the past or the future. The wall behind the older Santa was filled with old, framed, black and white photos of musicians of yesteryear.

Christmas Village is the birthplace to many famous musicians and we are very proud of our musical history, hence the Christmas concert every year. Declan was standing behind me looking at every picture on the wall. He wrapped his arms around me as if he was holding a teddy bear as he gave each photo its due. "These are amazing."

I just melted into his chest while he continued to admire the window. Not by accident, the music store is across from the barn entrance. We started to walk across the street and head down the "secret path" that passes between two stores and stretches from Big Tree Lane to the barn. The Emerson Barn is tucked away behind the strip of stores. It was designed that way to serve as almost security to the barn all while paying homage to it. The stores serve as the buffer that you need to cross to get to it but you would have to know the path leads there. The barn is mostly used only for special occasions so there was no real need to have it out on display.

Declan looked around with wonderment as we walked under the trellis and entered the path. Since the path runs between the stores I guess you could say it's an alley as well. The path is about one hundred feet long and there are beautiful murals running along both walls until you find yourself dumped out into a gulf of Christmas beauty.

The first order of business was the hot cider stand; one large cup each complete with a cinnamon stick. Hand in hand, we walked over to watch the families making snowmen. The kids were in their glory as they rolled varying snowmen body parts. Anna's kids were having snowball fights and making snowmen. There was a sled off to the side with an assortment of snowmen and snow lady appropriate accessories. Seeing the intrigue in Declan's eyes I pulled him over towards an available spot.

With a childlike chuckle he asked, "Where are you taking me?"

"Let's make a snowman."

"Really?"

"Of course. Haven't you heard the saying," 'Youth is the most precious thing in life; it is too bad it has to be wasted on young folks?'

Smiling, he immediately got to work. I had seen it in his eyes that this was something he wanted to do. With childlike enthusiasm his face lit up when he saw everyone rolling the giant snowballs. Who doesn't feel like a kid again when it starts to snow?

"I didn't really do any of this growing up. My foster parents weren't very, what would you call it, family oriented. I guess that's a pretty accurate description."

"Wow, I'm sorry. Let's try to make up for some lost time."

I walked over to the sleigh and pulled out a couple of hats, a couple of carrots, a few buttons and scarves. We made two snow people, one girl and one boy. The look on his face when they were completed was priceless. We stood between both of them and took a selfie; then I stepped out and had him get in between them and I took a picture of him by himself. He should have that memory of his first snowman all by himself.

I was having the best time I had ever had here and it hadn't even fully gotten under way yet. There is an amazing sound system set up around the outside that even extends to the perimeter of the property. Christmas music plays overhead up until the concert starts and then it turns over to the concert. For those who may step out for some air or for those that choose to continue to enjoy the outdoors can stay outside and listen instead.

The barn holds about four hundred people and there is a beautifully renovated loft that has a bar and cocktail tables set up for a more intimate viewing. I usually hang around on the main floor and mingle since Evan wasn't usually interested in having a cozy date night here. The lights started to flash indicating it was time to start to roll in if that was your desire. Reagan and Matt came walking over from the sleigh ride. She had a big smile on her face as she picked up her pace when she saw me.

"You ready for tonight?"

"Always! You?"

"Always!"

"Oh, Declan, I'm sorry, this is Matt, Reagan's boyfriend. Matt, this is Declan."

"Nice to meet you Matt. And nice to see you again Reagan. So, what is happening tonight that you ladies are ready for?"

Reagan looked at me perplex, "He doesn't know?"

"Know what?" Declan asked

Coyly, I replied, "I guess you'll have to wait and see"

"I'm intrigued. Shall we go in?"

Reagan and Matt walked in and then Declan took my hand, kissed me and we followed behind them. Declan took one step and looked around in amazement like the city boy that he is. The inside had a rustic look but it was modernized. It wasn't set up like we were going to be square dancing, nor did it have hay and saw dust all over the floor. There was a stage at the far end of the barn and seating around the perimeter. The center is open space for those who want to dance or just stand.

Looking around he said, "This place is beautiful. What is upstairs?"

"There are small cocktail tables and a bar up there."

"Shall we watch from up there? I'd imagine that we can at least have a better view and then it gives me an opportunity to have some private time with you. How does that sound?"

How does that sound? It sounds like I wouldn't even know how to approach an answer to that question. He actually wants to sit where I have been dying to sit and then he wants to make sure it's okay with me. Yeah, I don't know what to do with that. Reagan and Matt were going to stand up front so I whispered to her that I'd see her in a bit.

"I would love to sit upstairs."

We headed up and now I was the one looking around in amazement. I have always wanted to sit up here, better yet, I have always wanted to come up here. Evan thought it was silly. "What's the big deal? Oh, because everyone sits up here we have to sit up here? Please, I don't just follow what everyone else is doing." In all actuality my response should have been that no, we should sit up there at least once just because I would like that. I am sitting up here now, though. It was beautiful. There were blue LED lights that lit the bar area, some cozy little tables tucked away in corners and others lining what would be the bottom of the horseshoe in the horseshoe shaped room that over looked half of the dance floor and all of the stage. I looked down to see who else was here. Reagan was right up front, I saw Mrs. Eagan sitting alone on the left side of the stage, Anna was chasing one of her kids while the other three chased each other on the dance floor. Ruth and Flo were sitting about two rows behind Mrs. Eagan; there were a lot of new faces; guests of locals no doubt, I could see Ben adding some finishing touches on a prop. Candace came running in with her cider and grabbed a seat not far from Mrs. Eagan. Turning to Declan to thank him I caught him just staring at me.

"What?"

He laughed, "What what?"

"Why are you looking at me like that?"

"Like what?"

"Like THAT!" and I leaned over and kissed him.

"I am looking at the life in your eyes. I'm looking at the innocence in your face and the beauty of the total package."

Well, that was an involved answer that leaves me dumbfounded.

"Thank you for sitting up here."

"You don't have to thank me. I want to thank you for introducing me to this entire experience. I can't remember the last time I was this relaxed and had so much fun."

The lights went down and the first note was played and I drifted off into my own world. Christmas music is so cathartic for me. It reminds me of happier times when I was a child. My Christmases were amazing. The smells, the love, the feeling it ultimately gave me. It wan't about presents, it was just a feeling. A feeling I have never been able to recapture since I lost my parents.

Christmas seems to be a time where I get so excited and try, I try so hard, to make the most of the entire holiday season. Come Christmas Day, I end up in tears. It's so anticlimactic for me. No matter what I try to do to bring that feeling back all it does is make me feel like I'm on a hamster wheel. Add to that, Evan not wanting to give an inch to even try to acknowledge anything special about anything. It was as if he couldn't "give in" to anything I might find pleasing to do. Maybe it was a control thing; I don't know.

Again, it may come across like he was a terrible person, but he wasn't, I loved him, I just wasn't a priority. I will take part of the blame for that because I allowed myself to be a consolation prize. Evan wasn't always like that, he couldn't have been because I never would have started dating him. It was a gradual decline. Maybe I got too comfortable and let too many things slide. I just wasn't looking to play any games and I guess maybe my transparency wasn't exciting enough. Forgetting about him is obviously still a work in progress.

After the third song, I excused myself and told Declan I would be right back. The secret I hadn't told him was that Reagan and I would be doing a couple of songs. Reagan and I met up in the dressing room and changed into our outfits. We usually do a song together every year, except last year. I was planning that it was going to be a date night so I didn't sign up to do it, nor did it turn out to be a date night.

This year I wasn't anticipating having a date so I did sign up for it. Reagan and I were standing on the side of the stage waiting to be introduced. I could see Declan but he couldn't see me. He was watching the stage and taking it all in. As soon as mine and Reagan's name was announced I saw him look a little confused and then a big grin took over his face. We decided to be a little campy and had on matching red dresses. We sang "Where Are You Christmas" and "My Grown Up Christmas List" and we killed it if I do say so myself.

After a quick change in the dressing room I ran back upstairs to find Declan approaching. Our eyes met and I couldn't get the smile off my face.

I started to say, "A funny thing happened on the way to the bathroom…" I got as far as the first three words and he walked right up to me and put both his hands on my neck and pulled my mouth right to his. To say I was swept off my feet would be an understatement.

"You are a woman of many talents I see. You have an amazing voice, so does Reagan. You ladies should take that on the road and share your gift."

"You're too sweet. We used to be in a band in high school. Music was something we wanted to pursue, but I guess life got in the way."

"You truly are robbing the world of your talents."

Again, our bodies became one as we embraced. We managed to move ourselves back over to our table and Declan had gotten us each a glass of wine. The next few acts were a couple of local bands that play around town and they always take part in the Christmas concert. As I sat wrapped in Declan's arms with my eyes closed just envisioning everything I hear, they start to announce the next band.

"A little secret that the committee has kept under wraps is that we are honored to have a special band here tonight. They are currently on tour but took time out to come back to where it all started for them. Put your hands together and let's give them a big Christmas Village welcome home…….The Vexes."

My eyes flew open and I jumped up. It couldn't be. It just couldn't be.

"What's the matter? Are you okay?"

"Yes, sorry, would you like some water? I'm going to get some water. This is my second glass of wine tonight and I'm a lightweight. Can I get you anything?"

"No…thank you, I'm fine. Let me get the water."

"No, it's fine. I'm going to stretch my legs."

I paced around a little before making it over to the bar to grab two waters. Deep breath…exhale. Declan was engrossed in the show by the time I made it back to the table.

"I can't believe you guys got The Vexes to perform. This is amazing."

"Yeah, amazing."

The Vexes figured they would grace us with three songs, their idea of a Christmas gift perhaps….At approximately four minutes each; that was the longest twelve minutes of my life. They got a standing ovation, including from Declan.

"Wow, that was fantastic. Did you know they were going to perform?"

"No idea."

Trying to steer the focus back on us I asked Declan about the box again. I am really interested in what items he has from his parents. Unable to imagine what that even feels like I asked him if he really thought that if he found out this missing information if he really felt like that would give him closure. I'm not sure if it would give me closure or if it would make me sadder. Declan said in the box were a bunch of concert ticket stubs, a gold band, a necklace with a music note charm, a couple of old photographs and some love notes.

Maybe it's because I'm a female but it sounds to me like he has everything he needs right there. A woman can crack a case on social media with far less info than he is providing me with. Oh, Declan's red scarf that he wears all the time was in the box as well. Tomorrow is my day off so if Declan was up for some detective work, tomorrow would be perfect. We managed to talk a lot during the intermission. There were no awkward silences, we were still entranced with each other. This time I really did have to use the restroom. I excused myself and went downstairs to the ladies room. Reagan came running over to me as I made my way over.

"Can you believe it?"

"No, actually, I can't. Listen, can we not talk about this?"

I no sooner said that and I saw Reagan's eyes widen.

"What? What's wrong?"

She didn't say a word and she kept looking past me.

"Reagan!!"

As soon as I said that I felt a familiar touch.

"Brianna?"

OMG please tell me this isn't happening. Looking over my shoulder, there he was, my heartbreak.

"Evan."

"Brie, that was amazing. You blew me away with your voice. Why didn't you tell me you could sing like that?"

"Why couldn't you not be so self-absorbed and realize that she is an amazing multi-dimensional woman that you never bothered to get to know?"

"Reagan…I'd like to say that it's been too long…but it hasn't been nearly long enough."

Turning back to Brie he repeated his question. "When did you learn to sing?"

"I have been singing all of my life Evan."

"Why didn't I know that?"

I pointed to Reagan and she reiterated, "Because you are self-absorbed and never took the time to get to know her. And you make me sick."

"Reagan!"

"Sorry, that was just my input. I couldn't help myself."

Looking away from Reagan again, Evan offered to get me a drink.

"Let's catch up."

"I'm on my way to the ladies' room. It was good to see you. Good luck on your tour." I walked away from him and went straight into the bathroom. Reagan came in right behind me.

"Can you believe that guy?" She said as she went in the stall. He is who he is. Of course he thinks I would want to catch up because he hasn't considered for one moment that he broke my heart and that perhaps I didn't get over this as quickly as he did.

I went into the stall next to her, "He does have nerve, though, doesn't he, Reagan?"

"Absolutely."

Someone turned on the faucet and started washing their hands and I heard, "You just stick with that city boy and you ignore Mr. Rockstar. He will only break your heart again. Don't put yourself through it."

"Candace??"

Drying her hands off she said, "Yes darlin'…you stick with that city boy," and she walked out. Reagan and I met out at the sink and had a pow-wow about the current state of affairs. We determined that Evan was no good for me and that I need to ignore his existence; no matter how sexy he was. A final look and we headed back to our respective dates. Reagan and I usually meet up after the show if we get separated, by the front door. Our tradition has been that we go back to the café with Anna for a late snack, sometimes after a walk, but we always end up at the café.

Declan was talking to someone by the bar when I went back up. He politely excused himself as soon as he saw me and came right over.

"I'm sorry I took so long, I bumped in to Reagan."

He laughed, "You don't need to apologize or explain yourself. Relax. Should we sit back down? I'd imagine the show is about the start soon."

Yes, that's what I needed, just to sit back down and revisit where we left off before Evan ruined everything. No, let me not give him that power. Before, I allowed him to distract me. As the lights started to go down I saw Evan coming up the stairs. He has to be kidding me.

He wouldn't take me up here and thought it was ridiculous, now he is going to come up here when I am finally having my moment? I quickly turned before he caught me and just faced forward. My energy was completely off now. He manages to ruin my dates whether he is on them with me or not. Declan caught a glimpse out of the corner of his eye, nudged me and said, "Hey look, the singer from The Vexes is over at the bar."

Giving my best attempt at my impression of being unimpressed, I looked, said, "Oh" then turned back to the stage. The second half of the show was equally as impressive as the first. About five songs in, Declan excused himself to use the restroom.

Once he was out of sight, Evan sidled up right next to me. He brought over a glass of white wine for me. He seemed very pleased with himself and said, "If my memory serves, this is your favorite."

I couldn't help but chuckle to myself. I've never had a glass of white wine in my life.

"Wow, what a memory. What are you doing, Evan?"

"I just want to catch up and see how you're doing."

"Do you not hear the music? Now is really not the best time. This seat is taken by the way. Can you please leave before he comes back?"

"This is really beautiful up here. Would you like to grab a drink after the show?"

"Evan! Please…"

I saw Declan coming back up. God dammit! Curiously, Declan came over and he could see the unrest on my face. "Is everything okay?"

"Yes, this is Evan, he was just leaving."

Shaking his hand, "Hi Evan, Declan, nice to meet you."

"Hey…well, have a good night."

Declan took his seat and my hand. He looked at me and said, "Is everything okay?"

Smiling, comfortable and safe again I said, "Yes." There were only about four more songs after the whole Evan situation. He finally manages to be present on a date and it's when he's not supposed to be.

After the show we went downstairs and mingled for a few minutes. Declan spotted Ruth and Flo so he walked over to say hello. I thought I might catch Ben in something other than his work clothes but not tonight, because he was…working. Mrs. Eagan was walking towards Ben as I said good night to him.

Declan seemed to be very comfortable hanging out with my friends and being engaged even when I walked away. We decided to go hang out at the café after the show. Anna opens it up for just us and we treat it like its our own house and cook together and hang out and talk. It's become a staple of our holiday traditions. We all walked over together and Anna opened the door and let us all in.

Still conditioned to the negativity of socializing, I had to ask Declan again if he was okay with the plans. He was more than happy to be here and couldn't understand why I would even question it.

We pushed some tables together so that we had a big family table. Anna had already gone in the back to start getting some food ready. Declan had started playing with the kids so I went behind the counter to start getting some drinks out.

Anna came up behind me and as she grabbed some plates remarked, "Hmm, he's good with kids. If he can handle my four, he's a keeper." Yeah, he most certainly seems to be. The only issue is that this is so temporary it's almost cruel to continue to do this.

Armed with mini pizzas for the kids, a couple of regular pizzas for the adults, pitchers of soda and beer, Anna and I passed them around the table and we all tore into it.

I was happy that no one was interrogating Declan now that this was an informal get together. Although, I could tell Reagan was chomping at the bit. A few stern looks and she just grinned and sipped her beer.

"So Declan, what are your plans for Christmas? Will you still be in town?" I made a mental note to kill Reagan later.

"Reagan, I'm sure Declan has plans and as soon as his car is ready he will be heading right out. Ignore her, Declan."

"Well, actually, I didn't have solid plans. I was really just planning on working but then this car situation happened. It made it a working holiday."

Reagan got up and whispered as she walked passed me, "You're welcome," and continued over to the counter to grab more napkins. This was a perfect opportunity for me to expand on this topic. She lobbed this one to me and I ran with it.

"Anyone need anything while I'm up?"

Okay, so I dropped the proverbial ball. I walked behind the counter and washed my hands while I collected my thoughts. No, I'm just going to leave it for now and see what happens. Anna seemed relaxed for a change. The kids took a liking to Declan. It was sweet to watch his patience with them and you could tell it was genuine. Not only was Anna relaxed, but so was I.

There was no concern that I had to keep watch and make sure that my partner was happy and not bored almost like tending to a man-baby. He was a man, and was engaging and still kept tabs on me either by a knowing touch or a glance. This is the most relaxed I have been in a long time myself, come to think of it.

The conversations kept going and it really felt like we were one big family; a family of misfits, but a family, nonetheless. Anna opened up about her split from Mark and Declan listened with intensity. She was still angry but respectful.

For whatever reason, Mark just felt the need to move on…without discussing it with Anna first. While she was working all day and chauffeuring kids all over, Mark thought it a great time to start dating in his free time while she was working. One day she stopped home mid-day from work because she forgot something, and found him in bed—in their bed—with someone from the other side of town.

We are a small community, but there is enough mileage between here and the other side where she doesn't ever have to worry about bumping into her. It's funny the things you remember about traumatic situations. For instance, Anna can't remember what it is that she forgot that caused her to run home, but she remembers clear as day the two wine glasses on the kitchen counter with the bottle one quarter of the way full. She remembers thinking that means there was conversation, enough time spent to drink three quarters of a bottle of wine and whatever she is about to walk in to is only a moment of what really happened. She remembers the look on Mark's face when he realized the jig was up and it also looked like relief, but she has no recollection of the girl leaving the house or what she even said to him when she caught him.

Declan felt terrible. He now saw things in a new light, as anyone would. You just don't know someone's story and oftentimes people do a great job of covering it up.

Seemed like everyone was digging down deep tonight and sharing. I sat back down next to Declan and he started to open up to everyone and told them about his situation. The reason he ended up here was because his plan was to go about one hour past Christmas Village and do some investigative work regarding his parents. His work is also mobile so it was a win-win for him.

From what he has figured out his dad was a musician, possibly a drummer, and he was going to do some research in Woodstock in the Catskills. There is a club he was going to hit and hopefully something was going to come of that.

He had spent most of his time in Manhattan with any of his leads, this is the one that has taken him geographically the furthest. This isn't something he worked on full time, but recently he has been concentrating on it. I guess as we age and we start to question where we get some of our quirks and personality traits from. It can make you a bit curious.

"Declan, not to be a downer, but what is the likelihood that your dad has already passed? Have you considered that?" Matt asked.

"Yes, I've considered that. I have done death searches and so far, nothing has turned up."

"Gee, man, I wish you a lot of luck with this. That is quite a story. Is there anything we can do to help you? I'd be happy to lend you my car so that you can make the drive to the Catskills, if that would help."

"Wow, thank you, Matt. That is incredibly generous of you; however, I think I'm going to embrace the sign I was given and take advantage of these extra few days to spend time with this wonderful group of, I'd like to say, new friends."

"That's great… It will be great to almost be a part of this journey with you. I can't wait to see how it turns out and I hope it is everything you need it to be."

"Thank you. I appreciate that."

This whole conversation made me want him even more. To be able to be a part of this important chapter in his life is exciting. Before we knew it, we had spent about three hours just hanging out and talking. The kids were all passed out on the comfy window seat benches. Hoping the conversation didn't steer toward me at all, I grabbed my plate and was about to start to clear and Declan gently took my wrist and told me to sit.

"Relax, you work hard all day. I'll get this. I've been going on and on, tell me about your family. Will you be visiting with them on Christmas?"

I could see the look of panic come over everyone's face, specifically Reagan's, and it made me realize how uncomfortable I must make everyone feel. I'm so consumed with my own feelings I never considered the eggshells that I cause everyone to walk on because of it.

Reagan immediately jumped in and told Declan that we are one big family and that we, of course, would be all together. Knowing that is not what he was getting at and she was clearly sidestepping, he inquisitively looked at her and acknowledged that it sounded very special.

It's not a topic that is easy to discuss for me and since I keep myself surrounded by my close friends at all times, it is never anything that comes up. Everyone knows my story as I have lived here my whole life. This is the first time an out-of-towner has infiltrated the inner sanctum. Really, I don't even know how to address this hiccup in my little dream I am currently living.

Always the protector, Reagan interjected with her story. Obviously she had grown up here as well. Her life didn't so much go off rails as much as it simply just took a different course. Did she find herself being in a situation of being a teen mom or having her parents killed, did her relationship end due to infidelity?…no. Everyone has a story and their pain or struggle is their own.

Reagan is her own worst enemy. As energetic and full of life as she may come across at times, she is also the most generous, giving soul I have ever come to know. She protects me like a mother hen, but also will do the crazy things best friends do together. We definitely balance each other out, and tonight, she is carrying me through.

At thirty-two, Reagan was hoping to have at least moved out of Christmas Village. She was hoping by this point to be living in NYC and running a huge advertising agency. Her mom had gotten sick about ten years ago and she put her life on hold to care for her. After about six months time of staying day and night with her mom, she finally, at my insistence, reached out to an agency for home attendants. I was helping her, too, but this was something that needed to be done. She needed at least one day that she could just have to herself.

Matt was the home attendant they sent and he served as a distraction for her as well as support as she navigated her mother's illness. Matt started out just coming once a week so that Reagan could at least get out of the house or take an uninterrupted shower or just sleep in. Since her mom was secure with Matt, and with Reagan detaching herself from the guilt she initially felt, she had Matt come two days a week. One of those days Reagan would take to herself and the other day she tried to stay current with what was going on in the advertising world. Looking from outside the fishbowl was drastically different from actually being in the game and dealing with projects but that was all she could do at that point. I admire her so much because she was the one person, besides myself, that had planned down to the day she would embark on her journey, exactly what she was doing to do.

Without hesitation or giving it a second thought, as soon as her mother became ill, all plans went on the back burner. She never regretted that decision for one moment. She and her mother spent quality time together and she cared for her mother in her final days and was able to give back all that her mother had given to her.

Reagan and her mom were always close, as her mom was a single mom. It was just the two of them and they were thick as thieves. Reagan's dad left when she was about two years old so she can empathize with Declan.

As I said, we are a musical town and very artsy. Reagan's mom was a prima ballerina with the New York City Ballet and when she met Reagan's dad, she was only eighteen years old. Her mom was an extraordinary dancer, typically, a prima ballerina is in their mid twenties. This was a big deal. Her focus never should have been derailed, but it was. Her grandmother was so strict with her mother, she had her dancing from the age of two. With all of the intensity of her training, her success was not surprising, neither was her rebellion.

When her mom became pregnant, her grandmother threw her out of the house. She considered her a disgrace and embarrassment after all of the "work" she had put in to her, just to have her turn out pregnant. Reagan's mom never for one minute regretted getting pregnant. She considered it her greatest accomplishment. Luckily for Reagan she shared her memories with her and told her all about the ballet. Reagan knew her mother genuinely never regretted giving that up for a second. She was also given the privilege of all of the stories her mother had to share with her and she embraced them like the gold that they were.

Her mom and dad met one night when her mom had snuck out and wanted to feel normal. She and her best friend went to the legendary CBGB to hear some real, live rock music. Her mom was exhilarated watching the guitarist of the now famous Cold Blue rock band swing his long, luscious dark hair all over as he jammed on his baby blue Fender guitar. Her mother was a goner at that moment.

Immediately after the show, he came right over to her and the chemistry was intense. This was the excitement her mother craved but was deprived of due to the intensity of her training. Her mother's long, lean physique, coupled with her long golden hair and big blue eyes would obviously catch anyone's attention; especially the sexual prowess of a twenty-three-year-old up-and-coming rock star. Her mom was now driven on a daily basis by her need to be with Tommy. Living in New York City during this time afforded her mom a lot of opportunities in the evening that she could sneak out when her own mom would go to work. Tommy was just the bad influence she craved, as any young girl craves, but he also served up the inevitable same predictable outcome. Since Emma was so thin, her pregnancy began showing almost immediately. At two months pregnant, Emma broke the news to her mom and in one fell swoop she lost her job, became homeless and was nineteen years old and pregnant on the street. Tommy was touring with is band so Emma went with him until she was about eight months pregnant. Tommy was familiar with Christmas Village since he had stopped there a couple of times on tour. He thought it was a nice, wholesome, quiet place to bring Emma so she could start her life over and raise the baby.

It was a stop on his tour and a place he was familiar with, but like I said, a place Emma could start HER life over. Tommy bringing Emma to Christmas Village was his attempt at alleviating his guilt for his inevitable departure. Reagan was born June 30, 1988, at 9:00 a.m., just like the savvy business woman she is, to Emma Robbins, who was alone, at Kringle Hospital.

Tommy was on tour and didn't get back in time for the birth. Emma had already accepted what her future would be once she got a taste of what being on tour was like. She knew her future was that of a single mother and she embraced it. Her little angel was her escape from her horrible home life and she was committed to making sure her baby was loved and felt special and had the opportunity to be a child.

Since Emma didn't move to Christmas Village until she was eight months pregnant, she didn't have much time to make friends before she gave birth. Emma was overjoyed with the baby and spending every moment with her but she longed for a friendship too. With having been robbed of any real childhood and the opportunity to forge any sustainable friendships, Emma welcomed the knock on the door that cool afternoon October 8 when another young mom showed up to introduce herself and welcome her to the neighborhood.

Chapter Seven

Molly and Emma became quick friends. They were both single moms and both had daughters very close in age. Tommy would pop into town and bring some souvenirs and spend a day or two and then leave again. Emma had made peace with her relationship or lack thereof a long time ago. His phone calls became less and less and so did the visits. By the time Reagan was two years old, the visits had stopped and so had any expectation.

The difference between Molly and Emma was that Molly's boyfriend stuck around. Molly was a singer and her boyfriend Rick was the lead singer and guitarist for a very popular rock band called Electric Blue. Rick was about eight years older than Molly and he continued to play small clubs while Molly was recovering after having the baby.

Rick was head over heels for Molly and treated her like a queen. He embraced being a new dad, but did have to continue to play as that was their only source of income. All of Rick's shows were in driving distance so that he could come home each night and be with Molly and the baby. Molly sang backup in Rick's band and they usually did two duets a show together.

Luckily Rick was able to continue to work without Molly's absence being life altering to the band. Obviously their fans followed Molly's pregnancy and were very excited for their new addition and knew that the change in tour schedule was to accommodate Molly. The plan was that once Molly was comfortable enough to start venturing out with the baby they would all hit the road again and tour as a family.

While Molly was home, she and Emma would push their carriages around town and talk and build the close female bond they each craved. They were happy that their girls were so close in age and talked about them growing up as best friends just as Molly and Emma had become. Emma loved being a mom so much and was so secure in her role that when it came time for Molly to join Rick again on tour, she was okay with that.

Emma had never felt as free and happy in her entire life. Reagan was her life and she put all of her energy into filling her up and making sure that she was a secure, strong independent young woman. Emma wanted to give Reagan all of the love and security she never got as a little girl from her mother. When she first showed up in Christmas Village with Tommy, Emma had a little bit of money, but not much. Tommy was actually quite good about sending her money. Granted, it wasn't a lot but it was enough to get her through some rough patches. Unfortunately as his popularity increased, and the visits decreased, so did the money. Like anything in life, all things must come to an end.

Emma was a great saver. Even though she didn't have a lot of money, she knew how to manage it. The first thing she always did was pay herself. No matter how little food she had or how many bills needed to be paid, she always paid herself first and that was her savings. It was that crucial move that gave her the stability she needed and enabled her to move on from babysitting while Reagan was an infant to opening her own dance studio when Reagan started school. She taught classes during the day to the moms while their kids were in school and then she would go pick Reagan up from school, bring her back to the studio and teach a class for kids after school. This schedule afforded Emma the luxury of spending all of her time with Reagan. Reagan, of course, took part in the dance class, because this also ensured that there was some physical activity each day. They would then walk home and talk all about Reagan's day in school. That was at the highlight of Emma's day because it gave her insight to the only part of the day she missed with Reagan. And she got to see it through Reagan's eyes.

As soon as Molly came home from touring, she would head immediately over to Emma's house. The tours would only have Rick and Molly away for about two weeks at a time. Emma lived closer to town which was great for her to be able to get to her studio when that came to be. It was also a nice central location for when she was babysitting.

Molly and Rick didn't live far. You could walk to their house on a nice day or you could just drive if you were feeling lazy. Rick knew how important it was to make sure that Molly and Emma maintained their friendship, that was another reason why he scheduled the tours the way he did. Rick also didn't want his little girl growing up on the road without having any friends her age. The band was really established and finally got signed to a record deal. That was the culmination of all of the long nights driving, the writing sessions, the endless touring and the time apart from friends.

The first thing that Rick did when they signed the record deal was pay the house off. Rick wasn't your conventional, irresponsible rock star dad. Rick loved his family so much his priority was to protect and provide for them at all times. When Molly became a mom she was only nineteen years old and Rick was twenty seven. At nineteen, twenty-seven is a big jump. However, Rick never gave Molly a reason to ever doubt his love or intentions. Once the ink dried on that contract, Rick and Molly did not go buy a sports car or a mansion, they headed over to their attorney to draw up a will ensuring that in the event of their death, little Brie always had a place to live.

The next order business was to secure a custodian for Brie. Rick had no family and Molly had been estranged from her family for some time. Rick wanted to make sure that in the event of their death, Brie would be raised with their values by someone that they knew would love her as much as they do. Rick talked to Molly after she came home from visiting with Emma and Reagan. He explained that Emma is the most patient person he knows, she obviously loves Brie, Brie and Reagan will be best friends. It just seemed like the natural thing to do. They planned to walk over to Emma's in the morning and have the talk with her.

Putting Brie in the stroller they walked down Orchard Street and headed into town. They ran different scenarios back and forth between each other as they contemplated the possibility of her saying no. Like anything else, you always have your doubts, but in their hearts they didn't think she would say no. She loves Brie and she loves them. This was the first time since Molly rang this doorbell two years ago, that she was nervous and hesitant as she approached 15 Broad Street. Emma opened the door and greeted them with her trademark radiant smile. "C'mon in guys, why the long faces?"

It wasn't so much long faces as it was trepidation discussing not only the potential future care for their daughter, but the reality of their own mortality. At twenty-one that is something that is not usually even thought about let alone planned for. Rick was the Yin to Molly's Yang. Molly would have free spiritedly gone full throttle in to the entire recording and touring experience feet first. Briana would have been hanging in a papoose and Molly would have been rocking her as she sang, had her strapped in a car seat for any drives or flights and would have figured the rest out as she went. Shockingly, Rick was more proactive about planning. Talent aside, the success of the band was also due in part to Rick's significant business savvy and ability to negotiate. This poured over in to their personal lives which is why to this day, Brie has a roof over her head, a support system in place and she lives in a safe, family oriented, "happy" place. Brie was always the first priority to both Molly and Rick and, as important as music was in their life, it still took a back seat to Brie's needs.

Since Reagan was still sleeping, the ever maternal Emma took Brie out of Molly's arms and started loving her up immediately. Unknowingly she confirmed it right then and there for Molly and Rick. Emma didn't get to mush Brie up as much as she wanted, because, obviously, she was usually holding her own baby. But any mother knows the minute you get to grab up any baby for hugs and kisses, you do it.

Rick told the girls to chat and since Emma had her hands full, he would get them all some coffee. Molly always had a smile on her face and the first time Emma ever saw the life leave her face was when the conversation came around to the topic of death. "What's going on you guys, are you sick?"

They reassured her that this was something they were doing strictly to prepare for Brie's future. Obviously they planned on living forever as we all do when we have children, but we also must prepare for our imminent death. After they explained that this was just the next step in the celebration of the record deal, and securing their home life so they can freely enjoy their road life, Emma was, of course, on board. Emma made sure that it was clear to them that as much as she loved Brie, she never wanted to collect on that agreement. They all shook on it and then Molly got up and gave Emma a big hug and told her how much she loved her.

Next on Rick's agenda, was in his opinion, the pinnacle of his success. He asked Emma if she would babysit one night. It was the first overnight they were going to experience without Brie. Molly was a little uncomfortable with that, but she trusted Rick. He had reserved a suite at The Snowflake Lodge. He had Molly pack a bag for the night and told her to bring a pretty dress.

After they dropped Brie off to Emma, he assured her they would see her the next afternoon. They got in the car and looked at each other almost unsure of what to do. They had just dropped their missing puzzle piece off at Emma's and they almost forgot how to act on a date. The beauty of their relationship was that once Brie came along it didn't divide them, it only completed them. They were so in love from the first time they met nothing came between that. Their relationship was built on mutual respect and love for one another and each trusted the other's instincts. They had their critics because of the age difference, but that was something that never bothered them. It was something they never even noticed.

Rick pulled the pickup truck away from the front of Emma's and drove down the road. Molly was excited and couldn't imagine where they were off too. After a three minute drive, Rick parked in the lot at The Lodge. Extremely confused, Molly asked Rick why they were stopping at her job. He explained to her that today it wasn't her job but an opportunity to experience the services that she is responsible for gifting to others.

He got out of the truck and came around to open her door. Escorting her out, he opened the back door and grabbed their bags. They went up to the front desk and were greeted by the owner's daughter who was getting her feet wet in hopes of taking over the family business one day. Candace did a great job and had everything prepared for them as soon as they arrived.

Having never been in one of the suites, this was the first time Rick saw the unabashed glee on Molly's face as she looked around in amazement. She had never stayed in a room so special and extravagant before. Rick wanted to make sure Molly felt special and pampered since she worked so hard taking care of their daughter, him and working part-time when she wasn't touring. Really all she needed was to be with him, she never cared where they were as long as they were together.

Rick being Rick, he had a plan for everything. Obviously, Christmas was a special day and he wanted this date to be special for Molly but they also wanted to be with Brie on Christmas Day as well as Christmas Eve. He chose December 23 as their special date day, because now they could just make the most of the week. In his mind, they would be celebrating for three days straight in the future. Brie was now two and a half and they knew this Christmas was going to be a fun one for them. It's crazy how overnight you go from looking forward to opening presents to once you have children, even more excited to see them open presents.

The first thing Rick and Molly did when they got to the room was exactly what you would expect two young lovers with a two and a half year old would do on their first night alone…they took a nap. They felt like they had slept for a week. Molly was the first one to jump up and look around for Brie before she realized where she was. Rick put his arm around her and pulled her right back in to his chest. They slept about another hour before Rick woke Molly up by kissing her neck.

Before she even opened her eyes, a big sweeping grin took over her face. He gently rolled her over and started kissing her. They made love for the next few hours. Luckily since Rick made all of the appropriate requests and preparations, they had some chocolate-covered strawberries to snack on to keep their energy up.

Wanting to make use of every inch of this room they moved the party into the oversized Jacuzzi tub. No matter how much they planned on utilizing every inch of the room, since they move as a cohesive unit, they would have flourished in a closet. Molly sat nose to nose on Rick's lap kissing him in the jacuzzi negating the need for the rest of the tub. She slept lying across his chest and they moved as one, belying the king-sized bed that coincides with a suite.

Rick told Molly to get dressed up because they were going to have dinner downstairs in the restaurant. Molly was tall and lean and brought a form-fitting black sweater dress that sat mid-thigh, her long, blonde hair fell mid-back and her long legs were given more life by the four-inch heels of her knee-high black boots. When she came out of the bathroom, Rick took one look at her and just sat on the edge of the bed without saying a word. He was, for the first time, rendered speechless. Smiling at him, she walked over to take his hand and he stood up. They embraced and started slow dancing to the music their bodies heard when they connected. Stealing a few more kisses, Rick pulled away and finished getting dressed. Although they were parents to a two and a half year old, they were still musicians and soon-to-be rock stars. Molly's dress was elegant yet edgy, Rick put on his black leather pants and had a white button down shirt on. His bare chest was accessorized with multiple silver chains and a big silver cross. They already looked like the multi-million dollar deal they just signed.

It was nice to not have to ruin the outfits by wearing a coat or having the elements wreak havoc on their hair. Having the ability to just walk downstairs to the cozy restaurant was glorious. He took her hand and escorted her in to the beautifully decorated restaurant. There were two Christmas trees on either side of the stone fireplace, both emblazoned with white lights. Only one table set for two sat in the middle of the room and white silks draped all around the room and floor mimicking snow filled the empty space surrounding their table. A small square bud vase with red roses was placed in the middle of the table and classic Christmas tunes covered by current rockers played overhead.

This was a dream come true for Molly. She couldn't imagine her life being more fulfilled than it already was, but this night was a dream. Two glasses of champagne were strategically placed on the mantle and the remainder of the bottle was sitting next to the table in ice. Looking around and taking it all in, Molly remarked how beautiful everything was and wondered why the rest of the band wasn't there to celebrate with them. He took her hand and they walked over towards the Christmas tree on the far side of the fireplace. Molly noticed there was one red bulb in the all white tree.

"Look at that, look how strange that is," she remarked as they approached it. The red bulb was giving off an unusual blurred effect. Rick asked her what it was and she looked in disbelief. He reached from behind her, over her shoulder and took the round two-carat diamond ring off of the branch that sat in its little black velvet box and got down on one knee.

He held her hand as he looked up at her and pledged his love and fidelity to her. He told her that the first day the band checked in here after having driven for eight hours and he saw her behind the desk, he knew. He knew that whatever success the band was to have he wanted to share with her and he knew that he didn't want to leave the hotel that trip without making sure he had her number.

Cell phones back then were nothing compared to what they are today so any courting to be done was actual work. Anything that had to be said, needed to be said at the time. With his back towards the fireplace, Molly's face was glowing. He made sure she knew that he never had one doubt from the moment he set eyes on her that she was the one for him. He treated her as an equal in terms of intelligence, talent, gender…she was his partner. However, he did, on top of that, treat her like a queen. She was perfect in his eyes and she fed his soul.

He was the rock star that everyone wanted, but he saw no one but Molly. He would have proposed sooner, but he is a planner and wanted it all to be perfect. He wanted to bring it back to where it all started for him; the defining moment in his life. "Molly, you are my muse, my only true love. We are stronger together than we are apart. Our love created a life that embodies the best of both of us and will hopefully go on one day to do amazing things that make her happy. She will tell our story every day in everything she does. This ring won't take on its true beauty until you agree to wear it and know that I don't want to live a day on this earth without you by my side. Would you do me the honor of being my wife, partner in crime and forever muse?"

Molly stood there in all of her rock star beauty and slowly traced around the perimeter of Rick's face. She watched her finger touch every imperfection that made him perfect to her. She traced his full lips with her finger as he slowly took it in his mouth. Cupping his cheeks with both of her hands she got down on her knees so they were face to face and kissed him. Of course, she was going to say yes, but she wanted to feel every moment. Looking in his eyes and still holding his face she whispered, "I love you. I have always loved you and always will. We have always been one and although I know you are trying to show me the magnitude of your love, I don't want you to ever feel that you need to get down on your knees or lower yourself just to put me on a pedestal. We are one and we are in this together, face to face. I will say yes to forever, but I will not look down at you to say it."

Placing the ring on her finger, it now sparkled as it was intended to. He stood up, then helped her up. He took the two glasses of champagne off the mantle and toasted to a never-ending bond and life together.

Chapter Eight

As Reagan recounted her story, I sat there mesmerized. As she spoke of our mothers' friendship I realized she was narrating as if she was telling someone else's story. Because no one ever speaks of my parents around me, sitting, listening to Reagan ease into it made me realize how much I am missing out on. "Reagan, how did you know that detailed story about my parents engagement?"

"As soon as your mom and dad picked you up the next day your mom couldn't contain herself and told my mom everything. Brie, they shared all of their stories together."

A tear fell down my cheek and it was at that moment that I realized Reagan actually knew more about my parents than I did. I closed myself off from so much that I feel like I am missing part of my identity. We all learn from each other. Reagan didn't want to take credit for having the wherewithal to use her mother's dying time to extract any bit of pertinent information out of her. She said that if it wasn't for watching me go through life with no information, she never would have thought of it. Declan put his arm around me and said, "It sounds like we have more in common than we knew."

How did his coming here to find his father end up becoming me on a quest for information on my parents? Hearing Reagan tell the story of our mothers' meeting was cathartic. She described my parents with an insight that could only come from the depths of a friendship that could transcend time. I didn't even know that my own mother's recollection would be so precise. Emma and Molly really did have that undeniable bond that really couldn't be broken.

"Reagan, that was an amazing story. I'm so sorry for your heartache but you managed to put a beautiful spin on it."

"Thank you, Declan. We are all here for you as you continue to travel on your proverbial journey."

"I do have one question for you though, Reagan. You said that you started to care for your mom when you were twenty-two years old and that you met Matt approximately six months later. So, you were about twenty-two/twenty-three years old. You two have been together for ten years?"

Everyone busted out laughing, except Reagan.

"Not exactly, we have been together for four years."

"Oh, so that's cool, you guys were friends first."

"Yeah, friends, for six years before Matt had the nerve to ask me out."

Matt sort of shrugged it off. That's what I'm talking about with Matt. He is a great guy. Just maybe not a great guy for Reagan. She is a go-getter. She is strong but compassionate, deep but carefree. Matt takes six years of being close enough to someone whose mother he literally took care of for a year until she took her last breath, to ask her out. You held a dying woman in your arms while her daughter grieved beside you. You have the strength and lucidity to handle these intense human situations, but when it comes to asking a girl out who literally only spent time with you during her most painful and traumatic period of her life, you're tripped up with the signs? Some might say that is cute, most will say that is a wimp and a waste of precious time.

"Well, we are together now, so that should count for something right?"

"Yes, babe, it counts for four of the ten years you were lying in wait."

Everyone giggled, but for the first time I saw in Reagan's eyes something I had never seen before. She looked done. I could almost see the abacus in her eyes as she recounted the deranged courting period with Matt. She is not one to push things and she isn't someone who is in love with being in love. When you are in a situation where you are watching time go by and nothing else, it's time to start revisiting what brought you here. She waited six years for him to ask her out and then they dated another four. How much time do you need to make the next move? What more do you need to know about someone to know whether or not you want to take it to the next level? I would think that if you shared the worst moment in someone's life with them and still decided to ask them out after that, there can't be much more you need to witness.

All of this info tonight was a lot of food for thought for Declan. It didn't seem to scare him though, it looked like it gave him some inspiration. There was solidarity in knowing we were all struggling in some way. He asked me if I minded if we asked Reagan to look at the items as well. He said listening to her describe our parents made him wonder if she might unknowingly be harboring pertinent information that might be crucial to his investigation. Of course I didn't mind, because it was also going to be an opportunity for me to learn a little more myself. Incidentally, I truly appreciated him asking me if I minded Reagan joining us. That was a very telling sign to me about his character. As the time seemed to be rounding 1:00 a.m., we decided it was time to start to clean up and we talked about doing this again, in other words, not waiting until next year's Christmas concert. As Anna walked towards the back with a stack of dishes, she yelled over her shoulder, "Declan, I hope we didn't scare you off and that you might want to join us again for another night of, I guess, group therapy."

"I look forward to it."

Just like a family dinner, everyone got up and cleared everything from the tables and moved them back to their respective spots. The café was even cleaner that it normally is in the morning. Maybe we should do this more often. Declan took my hand and pulled me over to the corner and with both of his hands on my cheeks pulled me in for a kiss. "I'm sorry, I'm being selfish, but I needed that."

"If that's you being selfish…yeah I got nothing, go right ahead."

He smiled and gave me a big hug. "Let's help Anna get these little ones in the car."

Who is this guy? Evan would have kissed me good-bye about three hours ago, if he had come at all, and left me there. His reasoning would have been that I was there with my friends and that I was safe; as if that explains anything at all. All that really translates into is that he didn't want to stay and wanted to do what he wanted to do and I should be grateful he stopped by at all, and why am I making a big deal about him leaving? In a nutshell, again, I don't think it was personal, I think he would do that to whomever he was with. It's who he is. He will do what I want as long as it's something he has interest in. To me that means he does nothing new and basically the only things you know you like are the things you learned as a child. If you choose to never do something unfamiliar to you, how are you evolving at all? Isn't that what life is all about? I guess that is where we get the term man-baby from.

Anna looked so much better tonight than she did this morning. Maybe she was right and all she really needed was that cry. The kids are great and are all well adjusted, she really shouldn't worry about that. She is an amazing mom and never speaks ill of Mark in front of the kids even though I know every time she looks at him, she wants to choke him out. He is a good dad, he is just a garbage partner. I hope that she will eventually take time for herself and maybe find someone else…eventually. Her life is full with the kids and work, but she definitely lost a part of herself. She was an amazing painter and used to do exquisite work when she was in high school. The musical murals in the alley leading to the Emerson Barn were painted by Anna when she was just thirteen years old. The town literally commissioned her to do it.

After graduation, she was all set to go to New York City to attend Parsons School of Design. She never admitted to it, but I feel like Mark pressured her to stay home, so she did. He wasn't leaving Christmas Village any time soon, and he was too insecure to let Anna go to New York alone. He was afraid she would meet someone else and he guilted her into staying. Of course, I would have missed her terribly, but I never would have made her stay here. She should have been encouraged to spread her wings. There is no telling where that opportunity would have taken her and it's such a shame that she let it go for a man.

Of course, she has 4 beautiful children, but that doesn't mean she still wouldn't have had them. It's not like she got pregnant right away and was saddled with children. They were together after that missed opportunity for eight years before she got pregnant. She could have gone to college and came home and still sat around for four years before she got pregnant. He never even asked her to marry him. Of course, he is not completely to blame since she allowed this to happen. I think because they started dating so young, they just became too comfortable and codependent on each other.

Although, if it was Mark, she would have gone to New York, no questions asked. He doubled down on being a jerk by not only putting her in this position, but not even carrying out his end of the bargain by seeing it through to the end. She was always too good for him. Fast forward to today and she is constantly worn out, drives a run-down mini van, only owns clothing that is extremely comfortable or has some kind of food stain on it either from work or a child, and the last time she got her hair and nails done was for senior prom. Mark, on the other hand, is always dressed to the nines, drives the newest Range Rover, goes out to dinner about three nights a week and gets his Zen on every morning in yoga class.

Anna needs to start reclaiming her life. She doesn't need to get a man, but she needs to find herself again. She is an amazing mom, wonderful baker and a great Uber driver, but she is more than that and I think she forgot that a long time ago. Some think that I am not in a position to say anything as I have never left Christmas Village, but I have my reasons.

Anna was very appreciative of all of the help cleaning up and getting the kids into the car. I think the kids will sleep well tonight considering they got to run and dance a lot of their energy out. The crisp, fresh air from when they were building their snowmen also aided in their slumber. Hopefully, tonight Anna will also be able to get some rest and sleep in for once in the morning. We welcome Sundays as the café is closed. Tomorrow will be a big day for me because I can finally get a look at that box that Declan has been marinating with.

Declan and I walked back to the Snowflake Lodge hand in hand. He invited me in and asked if I would like to sit by the fire for a bit before I headed home. That sounded like a bad idea, so without hesitation I smiled and said, "Of course."

As we approached the front door I now saw the Lodge through new eyes. I imagined my father's hand had been on that very same crystal door knob as Declan opened the door for me. To think that my parents had walked these very halls and had stood at this front desk to get a key to their room. It was like Reagan's story was coming to life right before my eyes. Since it was so late I knew no one would be in the restaurant so I asked Declan if we could go in there for a moment.

Holding my hand, slowly we walked side by side into the restaurant. It was like being brought back in time. It's unbelievable that I had never been in that restaurant before that night that Declan invited me to dinner. I had never thought about it. Now I stood in the middle of the restaurant and looked around at the white lights embedded in all of the garland that adorned the perimeter. Although the decorations are different, the decor has remained untouched. Turning towards the fireplace, we walked over and although there were not Christmas trees on either side, there was lit garland all over the mantle. I ran my hand slowly along the top of the mantle closing my eyes while trying to feel the energy from that magical night my parents shared in this very spot. It's hard to explain the difference between this moment and living in the house I grew up in. Even though I lived with my parents in the little white cottage on Orchard Street, and I walk around that house everyday, there was something palpable about their energy outside of the home.

Feeling Declan's hand caress my shoulder, he whispered, "Are you okay?"

All I could do was smile while my eyes remained closed. I was phenomenal. To think I was standing in the exact spot that my mother stood as my father professed his undying love for her was a feeling that I would not even attempt to put into words. Cupping his face in my hands, I pulled Declan to my mouth. This moment just manifested its energy into our bodies communicating again. Standing in this spot was like a gravitational pull and an out-of-body experience. Declan's hands were lost in my hair as he kissed me. He pulled back and whispered, "Let's leave this place here for your parents, and let's go create our own."

We walked back up front to the fireplace in the lobby. That was exactly where he was standing when I walked in the night of our first date. I love that we can share this with my parents while still having our own spin on it. We got cozy in front of the fireplace and snuggled in each others arms. There was something about just sitting here and connecting without saying a word to each other.

This silent conversation was more informative than any conversation Evan and I ever had. He would use all the words, but there was no meaning behind them. They were nothing more than word salads and it was evident when I would ask a specific question about something that he had just said. The salad was always prepared and delivered but there was never any ability for a follow-through. His intent with the salads were nothing more than the anticipated acceptance of what was delivered as a pretty gift. When I opened up the gift by asking a question it was nothing more than a beautifully wrapped empty box.

Evan never understood that I only wanted to be with him. I had no demands. Other than wanting my love reciprocated and to feel valued and heard, I really needed nothing else. I was prepared to feed his soul, but he seemed more concerned with checking all of his requirements off his list without appreciating what we had. In his attempt to make sure he wasn't being emotionally or otherwise shortchanged, he forgot to meet me half way. I'm very sad that we are not together, because I know what we did have and I know what he...we were capable of. Maybe had he realized that it's okay to compromise, and to not be fearful that all women are the same, we would be in a different place right now. Men think that all women blame all men for their past relationships and judge them accordingly without considering that not all women are the same; just as there are woman who don't believe that all men are the same.

What I do know is that in this moment, I am at peace.

Chapter Nine

Luckily I was off Sunday morning, otherwise, I would have been late for work. I had the most restful sleep I have ever had in my thirty-two years. Slowly blinking trying to bring myself into the present, it took me a moment to realize where I was. We had fallen asleep intertwined in each others arms on the grey tufted couch. We had a really soft grey fleece blanket on us and the fire was still blazing. When I turned to look at Declan he was already awake and just looking at me with a soft smile.

"Oh my gosh, I can't believe we slept here all night. Why didn't you wake me up"

Tracing along my jaw bone he said, "Because then I wouldn't have been able to analyze every inch of your beautiful face."

On the table right in front of us was a tray containing a pot of hot water and an assortment of tea bags and two Irish coffee style cups. I looked over Declan's shoulder towards the front desk and Candace had a big grin on her face. I've never fallen asleep in a hotel lobby before, I'm not quite sure what proper etiquette is in regard to a walk of shame.

"Candace, I'm so sorry, I guess we were so wiped out from the concert last night we fell asleep chatting. Did you bring us tea?"

"You two just looked so cozy when I came in I didn't want to disturb you. I thought you might like to have something warm to drink when you got up"

She is so sweet. She is also a hopeless romantic. If her little antics help turn this situation in to anything, she can deliver all the tea and blankets she wants.

We sat up a bit and Declan poured the hot water in our cups and we rifled through the tea bags looking for a couple of Earl Grey bags. While they steeped, we tried to come up with a plan for the day to try to make some headway with Declan's precious treasures. After having a cup of tea together, he was going to go up to his room to shower and get ready while I headed home to do the same. We figured we would start here, I would look at the things he had and then we would call Reagan. Driving the hour-long drive to the club wasn't out of the question, but we had to look at what he had with him first. He kissed me and ran up to his room while I walked over to Candace.

"Thanks again, Candace. That was the perfect way to start my morning."

"He is so handsome and you guys really seem to hit it off. I haven't seen you smile that much…actually ever."

"Yeah, we really seem to have a connection."

"Listen, darlin', I have to tell you something."

I heard someone come down the steps and say, "Brianna?"

Candace dead panned me. "That's what I was just about to tell you."

The smile left my face and I turned around.

"Evan."

"Hey, what are you doing here?"

"I was just leaving."

"Why don't you stay and have breakfast with me?"

"I have plans, I have to go. It was nice seeing you again."

He took my wrist as I went to walk out, "Brie, please. Just give me five minutes. Let's go sit over here."

"No, not there, walk with me to my truck."

Candace peered over her glasses with a miffed look and kept pretending she was tending to her reservation book. She had his number a long time ago and she was not having this.

"Thank you again, Candace. Love you. I'll see you in a bit."

"Mmm hmm."

I didn't want the Lodge memories contaminated with Evan's energy. Not my parents' and certainly not mine and Declan's. I wish he was as attentive when we were together as he has been in the last two days. We got to the front door and I hesitated a second, I guess I was quizzing him, and then I turned the doorknob and he followed me out.

"Why the sudden urge to catch up, Evan? You weren't really too interested in what I had to say when we were together."

"Don't say that, Brie, you know that's not true. I love you. I will always love you."

"Are you kidding me? You come here now and tell me you love me? All I ever wanted was to hear that when we were together."

"Oh come on, Brie, you knew I loved you."

"That's your answer? How did I know you loved me?"

"Come on, Brie, do I really have to say it all the time? That was the problem with you. You had this checklist, and everything had to be marked off and every paper signed before you would open up."

"What?!"

"You know it's true. You were always mad at me. Unless I followed every one of your rules, you weren't happy."

"Oh my gosh, Evan, you really have some twisted recollection."

"You weren't mad all the time? You know you were. You were only happy if I fit in your little box. We were too different. When we were good, we were amazing, but then if I stepped out of line, you were mad and that was the problem."

We had finally arrived at my truck and I turned to him and said, "Evan, what do you want? You want to catch up, but all you have done is reiterate why you don't want to be with me and, frankly, I don't understand what point you are trying to make. We aren't together—you should be happy. Yet, here you are, what, wanting to be my friend and still reminding me on a daily basis why we can't be together? I don't want to be your friend. I wanted to be your girlfriend, but even when we lived under the guise of that, you still didn't acknowledge me as such. So again, I ask you, what do you want?"

"What do you mean I didn't 'acknowledge you as such'? I would stay over and you knew how I felt."

"Oh my gosh, you're still doing it. I can't do this anymore Evan. Go play your guitar and go be a rockstar and don't worry about me…not that you ever did. Give me the time I need to get over you, please."

"See, you don't care about my interests. My music is a joke to you."

"Are you really that out of touch and narcissistic? From everything I have said in these last 5 minutes, my broken heart, how much you hurt me, how I'm still trying to get over you, all you pulled out was that I didn't care about YOUR interests and YOUR music. Let me ask you something Evan, what is my passion?"

"What?"

"You don't understand the question? What is my passion? I don't know how else to phrase it."

"You like waitressing at the café."

"I like waitressing at the café? That's your answer?!"

"What is your point, Brie?"

"We were together for eighteen months and your answer to the question as to what my passion is, is that I like waitressing at the café. Why haven't I left Christmas Village?"

"You don't like to travel."

"You know what, this is good, let's keep it going, this is what I need. What is my favorite drink?"

"You like tea! HA, see?!"

Taking a deep cleansing breath, I turned to Evan and I said, "Look, I was always willing to stand by your side, to be your partner, to walk the walk. The fact is that we had the passion part of our relationship down, but when it came to having to compromise or, at the very least, take an interest or at least fake an interest in what I am passionate about, you couldn't do it. You are still standing here accusing me of not taking an interest in your music. When did you actually ever include me in it? You had no idea that I could sing. Obviously I'm interested in music. In eighteen months, you didn't know that. You didn't care to know."

"Why didn't you tell me?"

"Why didn't you try to get to know me? That's part of the journey. It's not just all supposed to be black and white and written down for you. You're supposed to do investigating and work. Relationships are work."

"They shouldn't have to be."

"Oh my gosh! Do you ever listen or do you only stick to your narrative and anything that I say just falls on deaf ears?"

"I heard you. I listen to you. We are just different. I can't just sit and watch Hallmark movies all day like you. I have to keep moving."

"I have never made you sit and watch Hallmark movies. However, I have sat and watched the Discovery Channel and learned how to build a motor for a submarine, I have learned all about most plane crashes in the last forty years, I have learned how to rebuild an engine for a truck, and I can most likely renovate my house by myself if need be."

"See, you learned things watching the shows I put on. I can't sit and watch that stuff you watch. I'm not saying you shouldn't, I'm just saying I can't."

"Do you listen to the words that come out of your mouth? You don't think anything of what you just said sounds a wee bit selfish."

"Why is it selfish? Just because I don't want to watch what you watch, why does that make me selfish? I shouldn't be forced to watch something I don't want to watch."

"It makes you selfish because we only watched what you wanted to watch and I never said a word. I watched it with an open mind and did appreciate learning but I also thought it would be reciprocated. You don't have to learn something from every show you watch. Some people want to just relax, veg out, be entertained or just feel good."

"And that's why you should watch those things, I just don't want to and don't see why I should have to."

"Because if you cared anything about me you would realize it's not about what we are watching, it was about spending time together and making the most of the time we spent together. You just chose to huff and puff like a petulant child if you 'had' to do or watch something you wouldn't ordinarily do on your own. Why are you here? What do you want?"

"Can't we be friends and just hang out?"

"Oh my gosh, you really don't get it. I don't want to be your friend. We passed that point. You can't put the toothpaste back in the tube. Do you really think I want to be your bud? Your friend? You're not even a good friend. If you were a good friend you wouldn't have strung me along for as long as you did. That is actually the complete opposite of a friend. Listen Evan, I have to go. I'm not your consolation prize. Oh, and, by the way, I hate white wine."

I got in my truck, shut the door and felt a piece of my heart reconnect. It won't happen over night, to some it may seem that it should be a no brainer. That isn't my concern though. I will heal in my own time and in my own way. If Declan serves as a distraction, so be it. I didn't fall in love with Evan overnight so I certainly won't get over him overnight. There were many amazing things about him that made me fall in love with him. Unfortunately, when you are at the end of a relationship all you can manage to do is remember the bad. I think it's a defense mechanism to make yourself hate someone just to make it easier to get over them. There is no point in wallowing in the good that there was if we aren't ever going to revisit that. All it's going to do is cause me pain, not him. He loved me in his own way, in a way he felt translated into love. I needed to be loved differently and it didn't seem to matter how many times I told him what I needed, he just kind of did it his way and felt that should be good enough. It's kind of like when you tell your kids to clean their room but they wash the car instead and then don't understand why you're mad.

I pulled out of the parking lot and left him standing there. I hope he isn't planning on staying too long, because I really don't want to be running into him in the Lodge nor do I want him killing the mojo in the Lodge. Figuring I'm about twenty minutes behind schedule, I moved as fast as I could. Driving up Big Tree Lane I replayed the entire night over and over again in my mind, causing a big smile to take over my face. I made the left down Orchard Street and pulled up next to my little white cottage. Running up to the door I caught myself before I slipped on the ice that had started to form on the path from the car. Since today was chilly and Sunday morning, it seemed like cozy clothes would be perfect for the day. Laying out an oversized grey sweatshirt and a pair of jeans, I hopped in the shower.

It seemed like I was in the shower for an hour. Today I was a little presumptuous and shaved my legs, I figured, better to be safe than sorry. Most women would not shave their legs in an attempt to not let things go too far but the way I see it, I'd just wind up being naked with hairy legs. Time to own it and stop acting like a little stubble will would have me stop him from letting this progress. The most time consuming part of this venture was drying my hair. With just a bit of mascara to finish off this super casual look for today, I picked up my phone to check my texts. Declan had sent a text saying he was ready whenever I was ready to come back to the Lodge. Grabbing my coat, and shutting the lights, I headed back in to town. Since it was Sunday, there weren't a lot of cars in town so I was able to park right in front of the Lodge.

When I walked in and looked to my right, Candace was still manning the desk.

"Hey, you! How did it go with you know who?"

"Well, I don't know. I don't know what was supposed to happen. I was able to have some closure, I think."

"Well, if that's what you wanted, then I'm happy for you."

"Candace, can I ask you something?"

"Of course, sweetheart."

"I know it was a long time ago, but do you remember the night my parents stayed here?"

She looked shocked that I was even bringing it up.

"Well, of course I do. Why do you ask?"

"Can you tell me about it?"

"What has you so curious about it now?"

"Reagan was telling me a story last night about when our mothers met and then she segued into when my parents got engaged. She piqued my curiosity."

"What did you want to know?"

"Were they really as in love as Reagan made it seem?"

"Well, I don't know what Reagan told you, but your parents were more in love than anyone I have ever seen. Your mother was so beautiful and your father was so handsome, all the girls loved him, but he only had eyes for your mother. They had a mutual respect for one another and they complimented each other. They both fawned over you all the time. The night they came in here was the first night I was working on my own. They were like family, but they were also like rock royalty. I was the one responsible for making sure everything went off without a hitch and I was terrified. Your dad had come in a week before to go over all of the details. He was a planner. He wanted to know who would be working that night and then he wanted to meet with them prior. It was a lot of pressure for a newbie like me, but I was up for the challenge. Your dad knew exactly how he wanted it to happen and we made sure it went down exactly how he wanted it to. I set the ring box in the tree that night right under the red light bulb. It was my idea to put chocolate covered strawberries in the room, your dad had wanted the champagne on the mantle so it was ready to be had as soon as she said yes. They looked like they were ready to shoot the cover for Rolling Stone when they walked down the stairs that night. Your dad was nervous. He loved her so much, he knew she would say yes but he wanted it to be perfect for her. Perfection for her was just being with him. That's all she ever needed and wanted. You know who reminds me of your dad?"

"No, who?"

"City Boy."

"Really? Why do you say that?"

"That night that you guys had dinner here, that was all him. He reserved the whole restaurant just like your dad did thirty years ago. He was the one that asked me to set it up the way you saw it. I didn't want to say anything to you out of respect, but that was all him and it was like I was reliving that night all over again. To see their beautiful little girl unknowingly mimicking their beautiful night here thirty years later, it was something to behold."

"Thank you Candace."

"You're welcome. Now, you just enjoy yourself with City Boy and let yourself be vulnerable."

I took my phone out and sent him a text that I was downstairs in the lobby. It wasn't more than two minutes and he came walking down the stairs. I turned to Candace and she had a big smile on her face. She gave me an approving nod. He looked so good. He too was dressed casually with a maroon hoodie and a pair of jeans. He walked over to get me.

"Would you like to have breakfast in the restaurant or should we order it up to my room?"

Needing to break out of my old habits, I straight up made a decision and answered him and didn't put out there the ridiculous, girlie, "Whatever you want to do". I was decisive and said, "Room service sounds great."

"Mr Hynds, you just give me a call when you're ready and we will have it sent straight up to you."

"Thank you, Candace, and please, call me Declan."

Declan took my hand and we headed upstairs.

"Are you hungry? I'm starving."

"Yes, me too!"

"Great, we will check out the menu and place the order then we can look through the box."

"Sounds good to me."

We went up to the second floor and headed towards the end of the hallway. He pulled out his key to room 233 and when he opened the door and I stepped in I was overcome with what felt like the air being sucked out of me. That is the only way I could think to describe it. The room was beautiful. The back wall that you see as soon as you walked in was all windows. The snow had started again and it looked beautiful. I looked around in amazement. To think a room like this is in our little Snowflake Lodge was astounding.

"Is this a suite?"

"It is."

"It's beautiful."

"Yes, it certainly is. This was the only room that was available when I arrived so I had to take it."

When I walked in I walked towards the window to see what kind of view he had. It partially overlooked the parking lot and when I noticed that, I felt sick. I turned and looked at him and said, "You oversee the parking lot."

He nonchalantly opened the desk drawer and took the menu out then looked at me and said, "Yes I do."

We stared at each other for a moment and then I said, "Were you looking out the window when I left?"

"I was."

"I can explain."

"There is nothing for you to explain."

"I feel like there is."

"Brie, I wasn't spying on you. I watched out the window to make sure that you got to your car okay. When I didn't see you right away I headed back downstairs, because honestly, I should have walked you to your car. When I got halfway down the stairs, I saw you walking out with Evan. I looked back out the window not to spy, but again, just to make sure you got in to your car safely. I had no idea that your ex was the lead singer of The Vexes. That's pretty impressive."

Switching gears with my attitude and getting defensive I said, "Impressive for whom?"

"All I'm saying is that his success is impressive, not impressive that you dated him. I'm actually impressed that he managed to land YOU."

"Yeah well, he's impressed enough with himself so don't get too impressed."

Declan laughed, "As long as you're okay, that's all that matters. I hate to change the subject, but can we look at this menu? Because I'm about to eat a glass, I'm so hungry."

"Of course."

We decided on a pot of tea (of course), a bowl of fresh fruit, some toast, oatmeal, and two mimosas. It was a Sunday brunch after all. What is brunch without mimosas? Declan called the order in to Candace and then it was the moment I had been waiting for.

Declan pulled a box out from the closet that was a rectangular shaped black leather box about twenty-four inches long. He brought it over to the bed and he opened it. I felt like I was intruding in his personal business. It didn't feel right. When I explained how I felt he reassured me that as of now, they were just items with no meaning. He had no idea if these things would even bring him any answers. They could just be trash at this point. There was no guarantee that these items were a direct link to his father or if in fact they served of any importance at all. The box had more items in it than he had alluded to, but that's a man for you. There was a drum stick, a few guitar pics, back stage passes, a stack of photos, a couple of letters and some ticket stubs. The ticket stubs were for various bands so they could have just been all the stubs she saved from any show she went to. He got up and walked over to the desk and brought back the red scarf that he has had on every day that I have seen him. "This was in there too." I looked at him as I took it from him. Rubbing the scarf between my fingers, I closed my eyes trying to imagine the journey it had been on. What could the significance of this be? It felt so soft, like cashmere, and it was special enough to be kept by his mom for some reason.

We decided to read the notes first. That seemed like the most obvious thing to do so perhaps some names or destinations were in them. There were only five letters in the box. Only one letter seemed like a love letter and it wasn't signed and the other four were like letters from what could be teen or young girl friends. The letters didn't have envelopes so it was hard to tell if they were mailed or if they were handed to her or passed in class for all we could tell. There was one letter from a Dawn and the only questionable sentence in it was the last one. The last sentence read, "What about Benji?"

"Did your mom have a dog?"

"Not that I know of."

I wrapped the scarf around my neck almost in an attempt to conjure up any vibe or inspiration I could. We pulled out the concert tickets and went through them one by one. Aerosmith, Def Leppard, Foreigner, Kiss, STYX, those were the ones that were legible. There were a handful of tickets that were torn in half and you could only see some of the letters to some of the bands. Ele, Dall, Tro were the three questionable tickets.

We were startled by the knock on the door, "Room service." I forgot all about the fact that we ordered food. Declan got up and let the server in while I continued to rifle through the box. Suddenly I wasn't as hungry as when I first got here. There were some amazing photos of bands that were autographed and personalized to his mom, Ri.

"Your mom knew all of these guys?"

"I have no idea."

"Your mom's name was Ri?"

"Yes, like rye bread, well, Riley," as he brought me a cup of tea, with cream and two Truvia, just like I like it. "Thank you."

He had his cup and sat down on the bed next to me. We both sat with our backs up agains the headboard as we tried to unravel this mystery. "Did people that knew her really well call her Ri?"

"Yes, I mean, I really don't know. I have only seen Ri written on things. She was mommy to me and I was too young to remember what anyone else would have called her."

"Well, I'm just wondering, did she introduce herself as Ri or Riley? If she just met someone and introduced her self as Riley, they would have autographed it as such. If these were autographed by people who already had an established relationship with her, they might just sign it how they know her. I think the trick is to try to figure out who your mom was before you start trying to figure out who your dad is. Where were you planning to go in the Catskills and what prompted that?"

"Well, I thought if I went to the club of those tickets that were torn in half maybe they could tell me what bands they were and then I would take it from there."

That actually sounded like a good idea. The three torn stubs were all from The Cavern in Woodstock.

"Have you called over there yet to see if they are even still in business?"

"I did and they are open today…if you felt like going on a little day trip. Again, I'd have to impose on you for your car as mine is still in the shop."

"Of course. That sounds fun. It's not more than about an hour outside of Christmas Village though, right?"

"No, it's a little under an hour."

Okay, I think I can handle that. We took a break and sat at the table and ate. I noticed Candace's influence with the small bowl of chocolate-covered strawberries as an added touch. We deliberated about what we have already unfurled from the box. I still want to look through the rest of those pictures. They mostly look like band shots and not necessarily individual pics. We will have to call Reagan in for sure before we leave. Maybe she can shine some light on this. It's so strange to think that Reagan and I are the same age and grew up together and she possibly holds the key to the information that Declan is looking for.

Chapter Ten

Now I know that dinner and brunch are two sure bets at Snowflake Lodge, I will probably be doing brunch here weekly and perhaps at least one dinner a week as well. We managed to shut the investigative work down long enough to make sure we were in the moment sharing brunch.

These were the mornings I always dreamed of with Evan. A low key, quiet Sunday morning just chatting and sharing and then taking off for the day upstate on a little day trip. There was too much stress getting up on a Sunday morning with him. He either jumped up and was annoyed that he was already behind the eight ball if he slept past 9:00 a.m. and then got angry at me for being upset that he was leaving. That was more pressure and stress on him that he apparently didn't need.

If he did manage to wake up and relax for a bit and turn the tv on while he had coffee, he already had me conditioned that he was running out at some point. I was afraid to even broach the subject of going out for the day because I figured that would trigger him to realize he probably already stayed too long. So, I would just sit and wait for him to dictate my day. That was my own fault because I allowed it.

It wasn't always like that. We sort of just devolved to that point and neither of us budged on our argument. Of course, I feel like I was right for the simple reason that I didn't think I was asking for or demanding much of anything other than attention and to be acknowledged. You begin to wonder if your separation anxiety is based on your past or if you are being conditioned this way now.

He felt that he should be able to have Sunday to himself because he worked all week and this was the only day he had to get things done. He felt that coming to my house every night should count as enough.

I begged to differ. I didn't feel like him coming here at 10:30 at night after he got home from work, showered, ate and sat and watched whatever he felt like watching before coming to me was something I should be grateful for. These were the things I wanted to share with him. He had his own space and then he came here and joined my world, but I was really not part of his.

My resentment built even though I told him all along I wished he would come earlier or I wished that one or two days on occasion he stayed here so that it felt natural and not so detached. Maybe that was the point I was missing, however, you can't blame me for misreading any intentions. You can't on one hand spend every night here and then question why I would expect a little more in return than just a sleepover with occasional dates.

He set the stage for all of the reasons he blamed me for his inability to compromise. The "demands" and the "box" I put him in was nothing more than the pressure he felt from the things I wanted, that he never delivered on. So, I got blamed for the request and treated as if it was something he actually had to do, when it was nothing more than him doing what he wanted to do; then being mad at me that he couldn't do it stress- or guilt-free.

That was then, this is now. Live and learn. My right now has a beautiful view of snow falling down behind a wall of floor-to-ceiling windows looking out over the clear pasture behind the Lodge. There is a beautiful man with dimples sitting in a cozy sweatshirt having a mimosa with me as we plan our day trip to delve into an important part of his life, that he is sharing with me. That is the stark comparison. He suggested we take the remainder of the strawberries with us on our trip.

We finished up and I texted Reagan asking her to meet us at the Lodge so she could look through the items. While we waited, we got back on the bed and started looking through the pictures. After the letters, I figured this would be the next best clue. Towards the middle of the pack we started to find pics with Declan's mom in them. She was gorgeous. Without seeing his father I can see where Declan got his looks from. They were dark Irish…Black hair and blue/green eyes. The contrast was striking.

I found a picture of his mom with two girls, they looked young, happy, free-spirited. They all had their arms around each other posing like this was a regular thing for them, perhaps, the best of friends. Another picture was of Ri and a guy sitting shoulder to shoulder but I could not make out his face. He was holding two drumsticks in his right hand and was resting his chin in the palm of the same hand. His face was completely turned towards Ri and he was just staring at her and she looked elated to be the object of his affection. You could tell that this was a comfortable situation, too. This was not a first meeting that was captured on film. It was fascinating to flip through these pictures and try to make a story out of them. It was easier for me to be more objective. because this was not my mother, I had no attachment to these people. Declan was looking at these things through a narrower lens than I was.

The first picture to go in the revisit pile was the one with the mystery man. Flipping the pictures over and checking for notes and inspecting each photo including background players was pretty time consuming. I found a picture that had Dawn in it so I put that in the revisit pile. Declan sat twirling the drum stick staring at the ceiling while he laid back in the bed. He was processing the information I was reporting on as I examined each picture. He said he has looked through these things so many times his eyes were crossing and was happy that I was taking a shot at it. There was a knock at the door and Declan got up to open it.

Candace had sent Reagan right up and she was carrying a cardboard cup holder with 3 teas in it. "I thought you guys might be able to use a caffeine boost" I looked at my watch and we had been at this for an hour since I had reached out to Reagan. "Sorry I took so long, I was dragging a bit this morning."

"Please don't apologize, I'm grateful you are willing to help"

"Of course, it sounds interesting."

We had piles of pictures separated all over the bottom of the king-sized bed. I explained to Reagan how I came to separate them the way I did and then told her what I thought about the letters. After that, I handed them all to her and then told her to have at it.

She examined them with the intensity a best friend would examine a cheating boyfriend's Facebook page. I knew this was the right move to involve her. She started to make her own revisit piles. She looked at Declan and said, "Give me that drumstick." He handed it to her and she started inspecting every inch of it. She then picked one of the pictures back up again and held it right up in front of her. Back to the stick she went checking every dent and frayed piece of wood. She grabbed for the letters again and picked up the unsigned letter and the one from Dawn.

I leaned over to Declan and whispered, "Watch this. It really is something to behold," and I could hardly contain my giggle. What we spent two and a half hours working on, she has reduced to a fifteen-minute session with all essential items in one pile.

"Okay, I think we have something to work with here for sure. My guess is that Dawn is a really close friend, perhaps a best friend, and her confidant. Benji is not your mom's dog but perhaps her love interest and a drummer. Look at this picture of the guy holding his sticks, there is a faint red stripe on the end of this stick and look at the stick in the picture, a red stripe."

"If these are mass-produced sticks, everyone has these sticks. Where are you going with this?"

"No, these are not mass-produced. Look at the details on these sticks. These are personalized. You need to find out who made these sticks and maybe there is a record of who the band or person was that ordered them. They are Promuco sticks, but look, part of the writing is scratched off, but it says 'ji'. Maybe Benji had his sticks made specifically for him. It's worth a try."

Declan and I looked at each other. She made sense. Okay, that was one to-do pile. "What else do you have?"

"Well, the only thing I can think of with Dawn is there has obviously been some back and forth and there must have been some issue or something came up and Dawn was asking Ri what she was planning on doing with Benji or how Benji was going to fit into this new situation. Was your mom a photographer? Most of these pictures seem to be band shots that they posed for and the other ones are really amazing, like she was on stage taking them, or at the very least, right up front. That could explain why she has so many passes and why she has a personal relationship with them."

Again, another great point made by Reagan. She took one particular photo and said, "I feel like I have seen this before. It looks familiar."

"Let me see."

I took a look at it. I know what she meant but I couldn't place it. "Let's put it in the revisit pile."

"So what is the plan? What are you guys going to do next?"

Declan ran her through the day, "We figured we would head to Woodstock and sit down with the owner and see if he could shine any light on the ticket stubs I have. I think that will really tie together the info that you came up with today and might have me headed in a better direction."

Reagan shot me a look of shock. "You're going to Woodstock? With Declan?"

Glaring at her, "Yes, I am."

Declan seemed confused, "Is that a problem?"

"No, I think it's great. Nice to see Brie taking a day off. Enjoy the ride, that's half the journey."

Reagan asked Declan if he minded if she took a couple of pictures with her phone of some of the things. She said she just wanted to look into a couple of things that are nagging at her. He, of course, said he didn't mind at all. We packed everything back into the leather-bound box and grabbed our coats.

Declan said, "Why don't you ladies wait here a minute while I run down and grab a container for the strawberries before we leave." That sounded like a plan. It gave Reagan an opportunity to grill me.

"You are really going to go to Woodstock?"

"I am."

"Why the sudden change of heart?"

"Oh, don't get me wrong, I am terrified. What am I supposed to do? I can give him my car but then he will question why I can't go and he already knows I am off today. I have no choice."

Reagan gave me a big hug and told me how proud she was of me. Proud may be a bold choice of adjectives for me, especially since I am still standing in the room.

"You got this. It's time, Brie. I'm sorry, but it is. If I can't get you to leave and he can, maybe the universe is sending you a message."

"What message is that?"

"I don't know, maybe that there is life outside of Christmas Village? That there is someone out there other than Evan that will treat you the way you deserve to be treated? That your parents didn't live their life and plan for your security so that you can sit securely home and not live your life? Brie, he is amazing from what I can see. Unless he is a real con artist, and got one over on me, he is worth the leap of faith."

As always, she was right. Declan came back up with a plastic container to pack up our chocolate covered strawberries for the trip. He also had a little brown bag to put the container in and he grabbed a handful of Truvia and some teabags and threw them in the bag. We were staring at him and then he looked over at us and said, "Just in case we stop somewhere that doesn't have the tea we like or Truvia for you."

Reagan looked at me with an all knowing eyebrow lift and said, "There is your sign. Evan didn't even know what you drank let alone knew how you took it. Enjoy your trip guys and let me know what you dig up. I feel invested in this and can't wait to see how it turns out."

She went down ahead of us and Declan looked at me and said, "You have amazing friends."

Yeah, I knew that. Now for the challenging part of the day. Getting in the truck and driving past the Christmas Village County lines. Declan grabbed a bag and threw in a couple of extra sweatshirts, socks, toothbrushes and toothpaste and blanket.

"Are you planning on staying over?"

"No, this is in case of emergency."

"What kind of emergency?"

"I don't know, that's why you take it. Flat tire, heat breaking, having the option to stay over if we want to, you know, anything."

"You're a planner I see."

"I like to be proactive. It's easier to handle situations with a little preparation as opposed to trying to back track and clean something up that was avoidable."

True. He took one more look around and pulled the door behind him . He did a test on the door to make sure it was locked. He turned to walk and I was just giving him a look that made him reply, "I'm from the city, not Christmas Village. We lock and check our doors. It's a habit that I don't see me breaking any time soon. Proactive, remember?" I shook my head and we headed downstairs. Candace was getting ready to leave for the day since she was in at the crack of dawn.

"I hear you two are headed to Woodstock. Brie, you make sure you have yourself a good time. You deserve it!"

"Thank you Candace and thank you for this morning and for brunch" as soon as I said that Declan lifted the little brown bag and said, "We have a snack for the road."

She winked at us as we headed out the front door. It was definitely a crisp day out. I hope we don't get a flat tire. My car isn't going to know what to do with itself since it has never seen anything outside of Christmas Village. With my luck, it will stop on its own at the county line. I gave Declan the keys and told him to drive since I didn't know how to get there. Figuring I would make a better co-pilot, I jumped in the passenger seat.

"We will probably get there faster if you drive. I can handle the radio and GPS."

Cautiously he gave me an inquisitive look. "That sounds like a good idea. I'm terrible with the GPS."

I knew he was just being kind. He found Christmas Village and he is a businessman, I'm quite sure he can handle a GPS. We headed out of the parking lot and down Big Tree Lane through town. We passed all of the stores we walked past last night before the show.

"Hey look, there's Reagan."

We drove past her and I looked over my shoulder. She was cupping her eyes up against the glass and was staring in to the closed music store. I turned back around and looked at the snow covered road that lay ahead.

After about two miles, we were off Big Tree Lane turning down a side road that would lead us out of town. This was a big step for me. Obviously, I didn't even have to touch the radio because as soon as he turned the car on, the 24/7 Christmas music channel was on. It relaxed me enough to get me to this point. He reached over and took my hand and asked me if I was okay. The electricity from his touch grounded me enough to make me feel like I could do this. All of a sudden a remake came on of Joy To The World…a very popular rock version.

Declan said, "Make that louder, I love this version."

"You do?"

Looking at my reaction then back to the road, he said, "Yeah, why? You don't like it?"

"Oh it's not that."

"What is it? I know that's not Evan so that can't be the reason."

"I like this version. I'm just usually quick to switch it when it comes on, because this is Reagan's dad. She doesn't really listen to his music."

Declan looked back at me and said, "Reagan's dad is Tommy Robbins? That was the Tommy in her story?"

"The one and only!"

"Wow. You all are really connected here aren't you? I guess I didn't put it together when she mentioned his band's name because I was just so enthralled with the story. Any other secrets you are keeping under wraps?"

"Maybe one more. We don't really think about it. Her dad left when she was a baby. She doesn't have him on the pedestal that everyone else does. Just like my parents, they were just my parents."

"You have never really spoken about your parents much. I don't want to push, but if you want to talk, I'm listening."

I looked out the window for the rest of the song. He continued to hold my hand and I could feel his thumb running back and forth over the top of my hand. As we drove over the county line I squeezed his hand in anticipation of what might happen next. We drove about a quarter of a mile past the county line and I realized at that moment that I have been corralled in Christmas Village by the invisible boundaries in my own mind. Declan just proved there was nothing physical holding me here.

"I've never been out of Christmas Village. I mean, from when I was old enough to remember. Reagan's story about my parents filled in a lot of blanks for me. I know my parents loved me more than anything and I can feel that I was a product of that love.

"I was five years old and my parents were heading home the week before Christmas from their tour. Like Reagan said, they took me with them everywhere, so that included tours. They loved Christmas so much they always wanted to celebrate it in Christmas Village. They made sure no matter where they were touring, it had to be close enough to home to drive just in case the weather was so bad that planes wouldn't take off.

"They really had everything planned, well I guess my dad did. In an effort to make it home in time to take part in all of the Christmas festivities, they drove home 200 miles from their last gig. My dad had checked the weather and it was supposed to be clear sailing. Not having internet access like we do today, he set off with what he thought would be a peaceful country drive in the snow.

"About fifty miles just outside of Christmas Village, an unexpected storm had hit. The roads were startlingly icy and my dad hit a patch of black ice sending the car off the road into a ditch. Always having me safe and protected, I was, of course, in a top-of-the-line car seat. My parents were killed instantly and I had no injuries."

Suddenly I burst into tears. That was the first time I had ever shared that story. Everyone in town knew my story so there was never a reason to talk about it. In fact, most of the town probably knew more than I did.

Squeezing my hand, Declan said, "Oh my gosh, Brie, I don't know what to say. You don't have to take this ride."

"Yes I do."

"Have you not left because you are afraid you might crash again?"

"I feel guilty."

"Why would you feel guilty? You were just a baby."

"If they weren't so concerned about getting back home for Christmas just to make sure that it was perfect for me, they would still be here."

"Oh Brie, you can't be serious. From what Reagan has said about your parents and from what anyone has ever said, they weren't the type of people that did things they didn't want to do or people that did things simply out of feeling pressured. These were people that loved with all that they had. If they wanted be home for Christmas for you, that was because of who they were. That was because they wanted to live life to its fullest. Because of that, the rest of their band got to be home with their families and not out on the road. Brie, just from what I have only just learned about them in the last two days, they seem like amazing people. If their daughter is any indication of the kind of people they were, I can assure you, they wouldn't want you ever feeling guilty or not living your life to its fullest. I'm so sorry you had to grow up without them.

Who raised you, if you don't mind me asking?"

"Reagan's story was accurate. Her mom was serious when she agreed to raise me. She raised me like I was her own. She was devastated with the loss of her best friend. I feel like I just serve as a sad reminder to everyone that misses them. I look like my father and sing like my mother. No matter what I do, I am reminding someone of them. Emma had enough love to give both Reagan and I. She gave me a good life and I will always be eternally grateful to Reagan for sharing her with me so selflessly. They were so close and then I get dropped on their doorstep. They never batted an eye and treated me like I belonged there."

Declan took a moment to absorb it all. "Brie, your life is a story in and of itself. Thank you for sharing it with me."

"Thank you for sharing yours with me. I just hope that we find what you're looking for."

Before I knew it, we were pulling in to the parking lot of The Cavern. With all of the conversation I didn't realize how quickly time would pass. He pulled up right in front and he got out and took a long, hard look before he walked over to open my door. I was still putting my boots on when he opened the door. He grabbed my foot and tickled it and then started kissing me. I wrapped my legs around him as we hugged and he carried me out of the truck.

"My boot!"

"I got you."

He carried me away from the truck as we kissed. This felt surreal, like something you would only read about or see in a movie. After a spin, he put me back in my seat and proceeded to slide my boot on for me. He took my hand and escorted me out of the truck. We walked to the front door and I stopped him. I suggested we just take a step back and take this moment in. We looked at the entire outside of the club. It literally looked like the outside of a cave. To think, this could possibly be a place that his father was in and that he actually did a show in. "Oh, hold on," he said as he ran back to the truck and reached in the back seat. He came walking back and held up the box, "I forgot the most important part." We went to the front and I pulled the long bar handle on the wooden cave like door, and we walked in. It was dark with minimal lighting around the bar area. It looked like it could use an update, but in the same vein, it looked very rock and roll.

"Hello," Declan called as we approached the bar. They were open, but it was only 3:00 in the afternoon so there wasn't anything going on. We saw a busboy come out so we called over to him.

"Hey buddy, is the owner around?"

"Sure, give me one-second and I'll get him for you."

I turned to Declan and said, "Can you believe this is really happening?"

"It's not happening yet. It's been a lot of dead ends up until this point."

"Since when are you so pessimistic?"

An older gentleman came walking over with a bit of a limp. He looked a little worn around the eyes but he was dressed like he was in the music business for a long time. Reaching out to shake Declan's hand, he said, "What can I do you two folks for? Can I get you a drink?"

"No, thank you. My name is Declan and this is Brie. I was wondering if you had a few minutes to talk. I'm doing a little research that has brought me to your location and I was hoping you could fill in the blanks."

He walked behind the bar and starting taking some glasses out and putting them on a tray.

"I'm not ratting out anyone's husband, or wife, I didn't see a thing."

"It's not like that."

He looked up and looked curious. "Then what is this about? You're not a cop... are you?"

"No, I have a few concert ticket stubs that have been torn in half and aren't very legible. I was hoping you might be able to shed some light on who the bands were that played here."

Looking around I was actually quite confident that Declan might get some info. This place has clearly not been updated so therefore I would assume any records kept would be physical records. This guy also looks like he remembers every joker that walks through the door and anyone that he has ever paid to play.

"What did you say your name was again? Declan?"

"Yes, sir."

"What kind of name is Declan?"

"It's Irish."

"Your old man is Irish?"

"Well, actually I don't know. My mother for sure was."

"You can call me Micky. Have a seat over here and let's see if we can't get you some answers."

We walked over to a corner booth. I loved the ambiance in here. You could feel the energy from the legends who played here. Looking around you could almost envision the greats as they played up on the small stage. Declan pulled out the stubs and Micky took a look.

"Wow, I haven't seen tickets like this in years. Where did you get these?"

"My mom passed away and this was with her personal effects. I was just hoping maybe you knew who these bands were since I can't read the name. I was hoping you maybe kept records of who has played here in the past."

Declan held my hand under the table and I could feel him giving me the squeeze that I was giving him when we drove out of Christmas Village. He was so nervous, we couldn't read Mickey at all and felt like this was the end of the line with the most pertinent information that he had.

"Son, I can tell you every band that I ever booked here in the last fifty years."

"Mickey, that is the best news I have heard in a long time."

"Ok, you give me a few minutes and I'll be right back." Mickey got out of the booth and walked in the back towards his office.

Declan got up and started pacing. "Can you believe this? This is going to happen!" He grabbed me and hugged me. "Thank you so much for coming with me. If it wasn't for your truck, I wouldn't be here and I'm so happy that you are sharing this with me."

I was too. Taking his hand, I walked towards the stage.

"Can you imagine how many people have stood on this stage? How many legends? This is the kind of stuff I love. I love to imagine someone, take Pat Benatar, for example, standing right here" and I jumped up on the stage. "She may have stood in this very spot." I closed my eyes and tried to channel her.

After singing a few lines to one of my favorite songs, I was lost in the moment. I opened my eyes to find Declan staring at me and two bus boys had stopped working and were staring at me and then I saw Mickey come walking at of his office with his eyeglasses in his hand.

He walked right up to me, and I realized I probably was not allowed up here. "I'm sorry Mickey, I just got caught up in the moment," and dropped down on the floor and dangled my feet off the stage.

"Little girl, where did you get a voice like that?"

"She's amazing isn't she? I told her she should be sharing her gift."

"You don't do this professionally? What do you do?"

"I'm a waitress. Well, I'm a writer…but I'm a waitress."

"No little girl, you're a singer. I only heard a voice like that one other time. Such a sad story, but you should take that on the road. Have you ever been here before?"

"No."

He took a long hard look at me, "You've never been here? Have we met before?"

"No sir."

"Hmm I never forget a face. I'll figure it out."

Turning back to Declan he said, "Now, for you sonny boy, you are looking for Dallas Trio, Troublemaker and Electric Blue"

I interjected, "Wait, what?! Electric Blue played here? One of those stubs is for Electric Blue?"

He held up a stub and said, "This one, Thursday, April 19, 1990, 8:00 p.m."

I grabbed it out of his hand and looked at Declan. "I can't believe this."

"Was this the only time they played here?"

"Only time? Sweetie they played here every week."

111

Shocked, I sat back down on the edge of the stage.

"That's it!"

I looked up at Mickey, "What's it?"

"You have the same face as the lead singer in Electric Blue."

I looked at him and my eyes filled up.

"Jesus, Mary and St. Joseph. Brianna...you're Baby Blue, aren't you? I knew that voice when you were singing."

"Baby Blue?"

In that moment I saw a gruff, old school, Irish club owner reduced to tears.

"That's what I would call you. You hung out with me while your parents did their set. You and I were the best of friends. Now look at you. All grown up. It's terrible what happened to your parents." He pulled a handkerchief out and wiped his eyes and then blew his nose. "I'm sorry, I don't mean to upset you."

I am so dumbfounded, I don't even know what to say. Declan came over and put his arm around me. He said, "You have to excuse us. This was just a lot of information and it was a lot more than we were expecting to encounter."

"Would you like me to give you a tour of the backstage area?"

I jumped up, "Yes, please."

Declan took my hand and we followed Mickey to the back. The hallway was lined with photos from the bands that played there. "Come here, I want to show you something." Still trying to check out all the pictures, Mickey stopped in front of one and smiled. We looked up and there were my parents on stage together. And then Mickey said, "This one is my favorite." It was a candid shot of my parents backstage with me on my mom's lap. I had never seen these before, and they were fabulous.

"Would you like to have them?"

Jerking my head toward him I said, "Are you serious?"

"You have no idea how happy you have made me. To see my little Baby Blue again, and to know that these pictures will be with their proper owner, I couldn't ask for more."

Declan took them down for me and Mickey had one of the busboys bring over a bag to wrap them in. Never did I imagine that today would end up the way it did.

"Declan, I feel like I Bogarted your adventure. We were supposed to be getting info for you."

"Brie, this day has been incredible. I got my info, and now I can go back to the Lodge and research more."

I had to ask, "Mickey, one last thing before we leave, do you know a Benji?"

He looked confused. "Benji?"

"Yeah, any of your bands have a Benji?"

"Not that I can recall."

I took the box from Declan, and went through the pictures. "What about her? Do you remember seeing her before?"

"Boy, you two are really taking me down memory lane today aren't you?" He smiled and then said, "That's Ri."

"You know her?"

"Sure...she took a lot of those pictures you just saw on the wall. She would volunteer to photograph depending on who was playing and then I'd let her in for free. Her pictures were so good, it was a win-win for me. I didn't lose any money letting her in and then I got these fantastic pictures. How do you know her?"

Declan said, "She's my mother."

"Well, I'll be damned" and he stepped back and took a long hard look at Declan. "You are one handsome son of a gun. Did you say that she passed away?"

"She did."

"That's terribly sad...I'm sorry, son. She too was a wonderful woman."

"Did you ever notice her hanging around with any guy in particular?"

113

"No, not when she was here. She hung around with her friend Dawn if she came with anyone at all. She was very interested in music, but her passion was her photography. She was serious about it. That's not to say she didn't like some of the boys, I just never saw her take an interest in anyone in particular. I wish there was something more I could tell you."

"Mickey, you have no idea how helpful you were. If we find nothing else out, you have changed mine and Brie's life forever."

As if a lightbulb went on, Mickey said, "Follow me." Declan and I looked at each other and then eagerly followed Mickey backstage again. We walked further down the hall than before, passing the classic shots and the now two empty places on the wall. Slowing down and now searching for something in particular, he said, "Ah, here we are. This is what I guess you young ones would call today a selfie." We looked up and there was a black and white photo of Mickey and Ri. Her arm was extended so she had taken the pic of the two of them. Mickey seemed to be getting his memory triggered.

"You know, I haven't had to think about any of this for many years, but since you guys are here, I'm trying my best to give you all the information I have. This picture was actually taken on the date of that stub that you have there. The night your parents played. I distinctly remember because that was the first time she had ever met your parents and I introduced them. This night stands out so much because it was the last time I saw her. She took those photos of your parents that night and she took this one. She mailed me those photos which was very unusual. She always brought them in and this time she mailed them and I never heard from her again."

"She was sick. She passed away the following year."

Mickey took the picture of him and Ri down and said, "Please take this. I have my memories. This is yours."

After a long hug, we told Mickey we would be in touch and let him know how this journey ends. We couldn't thank him enough. He gave us so much more than we ever could have imagined. Just talking with someone who knows our parents makes it feel so real.

Chapter Eleven

The drive back had a way different vibe than going there. We were both handed a huge serving of information that I don't think either of us were prepared for. Declan was thrilled with what he found out and the pictures were just an added bonus. I'm thinking that the next order of business should be to try to find her friend Dawn. The girlfriends usually know more about things than anyone else. Mickey didn't know anything about Dawn other than seeing her on occasion. That may be a task we need to take back to the drawing board. It was about 5:00 p.m. and Declan had spotted a cute diner when we were on our way up and asked if I wanted to stop in for dinner. Since this was already like a dream, and I was trying to remain asleep, of course, I agreed. He pulled over into the plowed parking lot and found a spot on the side of the diner. I was surprised to see it so packed but what do I know since I only walk around my town on a Sunday.

The old style diner door bell rang as we walked in and the waitress called from behind the counter, "Take a seat anywhere and I'll right with you." This place was amazing. This was the exact type country diner I would watch in my Christmas movies. I spun around quickly to check out a little detail as we walked to a booth. Declan wondered what was wrong but I told him I just had to see if that bell on the door had a little sprig of holly on it; of course it did. My dream was manifesting itself into reality rather quickly. It's the little details that make the difference for me. We grabbed an available booth by the window and we were greeted almost immediately by an extremely effervescent young waitress. She gave us two waters in the notorious amber diner glasses and pulled a pen out of her hair and her pad out of her apron. This was amazing. I couldn't help but stare wide-eyed while I captured her every move. "Do y'all know what you want or do you need a minute? I can tell you the specials if you're interested." I laughed to myself, this was everything. I needed this to continue, so I, of course, had to bite.

"That would be great…Erin," as I peered at the classic plastic name tag, which was right next to the poinsettia flower pinned to her uniform.

Smiling an adorable smile as if she was thrilled to be able to extend herself for us, she said, "We have meatloaf with some mashed potatoes and gravy, we have the chef's special-Goulash and we also have spaghetti and meatballs. They all come with a salad, and then of course, we have our regular menu. With the regular menu you can choose soup or salad and our soup of the day is split pea."

I almost wanted to order from the specials just because of the way she presented them. However, I knew if I ate any of that, I would probably end up in Kringle General because my stomach couldn't handle it. We went off the regular menu and both got turkey burgers with salad instead of fries and stuck with the water. While we waited for our food we talked about our next move. I had an epiphany while we were conjuring up ideas. This was the only diner we saw on the stretch of road. What is the likelihood in its heyday, that the crowd from The Cavern would hit the diner and hang out here after the shows? The Cavern served food but usually a crowd will hit a diner after any kind of social event just to let loose and eat unhealthy food. "What are the chances that someone here would know your mom?"

"I don't know Brie, I mean look around. This is a young staff. I think it's a long shot. I don't see anyone here that looks like they are a day over twenty-five."

"That's true, but it's also 5:00. A lot of times the older staff gets the day shift due to seniority or just because they are looking to get out of the house and aren't necessarily working because they can't make their bills."

"That's a good point. I mean, the answer is always no unless you ask, right?"

Erin came over with our plates and she still had that broad beautiful smile on her face. You could see she was destined for something far greater than reading off a specials menu.

"Now, y'all leave room for our homemade apple pie."

"Erin, can I ask you something?"

"Of course, darlin'."

"Are you familiar with The Cavern?"

"Oh sure, they keep us in business."

I peered over at Declan and gave him an all knowing smirk and wink. "How so?"

"We are a 24-hour diner, anytime they have a show, we are packed with posers, wannabes and fans and, oftentimes, celebrities."

"Really? Is this something new?"

"Oh no, this is what this diner is known for. We are a small town, but to The Cavern attendees, we are a staple in the community."

"I know you are a bit young, but might there be anyone that works here that we might be able to talk to about some fans, or celebrities from say, the late '80s early '90s?"

"Hmm, the only person that may be able to help you would be my mom."

"Great, is there any way we could impose on you to set up a meeting for us? It really is quite important."

"Sure, if you just give her five minutes I'll send her out, she is finishing up a phone call."

"She's here?"

Giggling, "Of course, she owns this place."

Declan and I could not believe our luck. I grabbed the keys from Declan and ran out to the truck. Rifling through our belongings, I grabbed the pictures that Mickey had just given us and the box that Declan brought with all of his items. The pictures were a little dusty and were in 11x14 frames. I made it back to the table before Erin's mom got there. Declan and I held hands hoping our combined energy would summon the luck we so desperately needed. A tall beautiful brunette with long thick hair came walking over to us. My heart was pounding, I just had a gut feeling. She had on faded, form-fitting Levis, a simple white t-shirt and her makeup-free face made her look like Erin's sister. She looked rock and roll.

"Hi guys, Erin said you wanted to see me? Was everything okay?"

"Hi, my name is Declan and this is Brie."

"Declan? Wow. You don't hear that name too often."

"My mother was unique. We were in the area just trying to find out some information and we were wondering if you might be able to help us. We were just wondering how familiar you were with the crowd or bands that played at The Cavern, say, in the late '80s early '90s."

A big smile took over her face. "Wow, The Cavern. Our big crowds are an overflow from there but no one has ever asked me about the earlier days. It's usually just kids or the young ones Erin's age that blow through here. I just live vicariously through them now."

"If you have some time we would love to talk to you for a few minutes, if that's okay?"

"Sure, that sounds great. It would be nice to be able to reminisce with someone. What information are you guys looking for specifically?"

I opened up the box and pulled out a picture of Ri with two other girls. The leggy brunette took the photo and she looked like she saw a ghost. Without saying a word she slid in the booth next to me. She looked back and forth between us and said, "Where did you get this?"

Declan hesitated and said, "Do you know them?"

She never took her eyes off the picture and smiled a solemn smile and said, "Very well."

We waited for what we tried to figure might be an appropriate amount of time before quietly asking again, "Can you tell us who they are?"

She looked up with a tear in her eye, "That's me, Ri and Gi."

It wasn't until I felt Declan tighten his grip that I realized we had our legs intertwined under the table.

Trying to be as respectful to her feelings as we could while still trying to delve into this mystery, I said, "And you are?"

She shook herself out of the nostalgia and said, "Oh, I'm so sorry, guys, I'm Dawn."

"Dawn?! We have been looking for you."

"You have? Why? And why do you have this picture?"

"It was my mother's."

"Your mother?" And then it hit her. "Declan??" She reached over and cupped his face and looked into his eyes. "Oh my gosh, it is you."

The tears streamed down her face and I think they went between sorrow and joy.

"What brought you here?"

She took her phone out of her pocket and said, "I just have to take a picture of this." She then looked up at us and said, "I never thought I'd ever see you again."

"You knew me as a child?"

She laughed, "Knew you, darlin', I changed your diapers. Your mom and I were best friends and spent all of our time together. When she died it was like a part of me died. I wish I could have taken you when she passed, but I could barely take care of myself at that point. It wouldn't have been fair to you. She wanted you to have a good life."

"Why didn't she send me to live with my father?"

"Oh boy, honey, I never imagined I would be the one to have to have this conversation with you. She was never supposed to die. She was young when she got pregnant. She and your dad were head over heels in love. Your dad was amazing. His star was rising with his band and when she found out she was pregnant, she was afraid to tell her parents, and even more afraid to tell your dad. I'm the only one that knew she was pregnant.

"She moved to the city and didn't tell your dad because she knew if she told him, he would let his career go. She knew he worked his whole life for music and didn't want to be the reason he didn't make it. She felt he would eventually grow resentful of her and she couldn't bear the thought of them not loving each other forever. She was a strong woman, but she had a soft heart.

"We had many long talks going back and forth about what to do. Losing your father at all would destroy her and she was riddled with guilt not telling him about you. Honestly, she didn't know what she was doing, but tried the best that she could with what she had.

"I know that she did try to find your father the last year of her life. She went to a couple of places she knew he would be playing but she never got to see him. The last show she went to, he had someone sitting in for him because he had a scheduling conflict. He would sit in with other bands, you know musicians, they can't say no to a gig. So, she didn't actually get to make the contact. When she found out she was sick, she was searching for him so that you would be left with family. But her illness progressed so quickly, it never happened."

"What was my father's name?"

"Benji Hoke."

"What ever happened to him? Did he become a big rock star like she thought he would be?"

"I really don't know what ever came of him. One of the bands he was in, the one that was going to make a name for him was struck with tragedy so I don't know if he wound up full time with one of the other bands he was playing with or if he just dropped off the face of the earth."

"That's sad…for everyone. What was the name of the band that was struck with tragedy?"

She still couldn't take her eyes off of that picture.

"I loved your mom so much. We had the best times together." She excused herself and reached across me and took a napkin out of the '50s style napkin dispenser and blew her nose. "I'm sorry, this is all a bit overwhelming, the band was Electric Blue."

It was like a shot in the gut. I had been pummeled all day with information that I never anticipated ever being privy to.

"Molly and Rick, well, Rick was the lead singer. I always say them as one because that was what you thought when you saw them. Rick and Molly were driving home during a storm to be home for Christmas and they were in a terrible car accident. Their baby girl survived, but, unfortunately, Rick and Molly were killed instantly. There was no band after that. Rick and Molly were the heart of the band and no one would ever consider doing anything without them in that capacity."

Owning the reality, I said, "I'm the baby girl."

Covering her mouth she said, "Oh dear God,, this is insane. You're Baby Blue? You were a fixture at any show they did. Old Mickey at The Cavern used to call you Baby Blue."

"We just spent the early part of the afternoon with Mickey. He filled in a lot of the missing pieces. It was by chance that we found you. Can I ask you one other question?"

"Of course, anything."

I pulled out the letter Ri saved from Dawn out of Declan's box. "What did you mean when you wrote this?"

"Oh my gosh, she saved my note?"

"She saved a few things that were special to her."

She read the last line and then looked up at Declan. "I was asking her what she was going to do with Benji, meaning, was she going to tell him about you."

Just in case she had anything else to add I showed her the ticket stubs. "Do these mean anything to you?"

"Wow...sure. These were the times she went to The Cavern to try to catch your dad. The last time she went there was for the Electric Blue show, but he wasn't there that night. That was the first time she ever met Rick and Molly."

We were confused and Declan asked, "If she had a relationship with Benji, and he was in their band, how is it that the first time they met was the last show?"

"Ri met Benji when he was playing with Dallas Trio and she followed them around. This was a last ditch effort to find Benji when she went to The Cavern that night." Looking back and forth at us, and smiling she said, "Maybe it was fate. All things happen for a reason."

We showed her the pictures that Mickey gave us and showed her the pictures in the box. She wasn't able to give us any more info than she already had but she definitely enjoyed looking at everything we had. It brought back great memories for her and she told us that any time we wanted to stop by and feel closer to our parents, that she was always there. Erin came over with the check and Dawn ripped it out of her hand. She stood up and said to Erin, "Go get our friends some apple pie à la mode. And you two...give me a hug."

After a long hug, long enough so that I could feel as though I had just connected with my parents, she took a step back and looked at us. "Dang, if you aren't the picture of your father, and you, Declan, you have your mom's hair but your father's eyes. Those baby blues are what did your mother in. When you find your father, and I hope that you do, don't be angry with him. I can assure you, he had no idea. In the same vein, don't be angry with your mother. We do the best that we can do as parents and the rest is praying. Anything that was done, was done out of love. She loved you more than anything in this world and she loved your father more than anyone. After your father, there was no one else. He was the only one for her."

To say today was cathartic would be an understatement. As we got up to leave I looked back and saw Declan slide a $100 bill under my water glass for Erin. That's who he is. It was dark by the time we got back in the truck. Thank God it wasn't snowing. I didn't feel the need to test out all of my fears in one day. Baby steps.

Declan and I were both so thrilled to have gotten all of this information. Now we still had to digest it. Just about ten miles out of Christmas Village, my phone started blowing up. Being so wrapped up in everything going on today I never even realized I wasn't getting any texts. Apparently, there was no reception and that can make for a crazed Reagan if she is looking to tell me something. Five missed calls and ten texts just saying, "Call me." Luckily I know how her mind works and I realize that this is just gossip and that there is no emergency. I asked Declan if he minded if I just returned her call just to double check.

"Hey Reagan, what's with the SOS?"

"I have been trying to get you for hours."

"I see that. I'm sorry, there was no reception. I just got it now. We are almost home, what's up?"

"I have a lead on Declan's dad."

I peered over at Declan, "You do?"

"Yes, wait, did you already find him?"

"No, but we have so much information it's too much to go over on the phone."

"Okay, good. I'm glad you guys made some headway. Listen, I think you guys should check out the music store in town. Obviously it was closed today but the pictures in the window in the display caught my eye. It might be worth a trip into the store to talk to Al. He has been there forever and there are a lot of pictures hanging up in there. Maybe he played here. Maybe he can put a name to the face in your pictures also."

"That's a great idea Reagan, thank you. Oh, by the way, we do finally have a name."

"You're kidding!"

"No, his name is Benji Hoke."

"That's fantastic. Be careful getting home and let's meet up tomorrow because I'm dying to find out what else you guys got."

"You got it. Love you. Talk to you tomorrow."

"Everything okay with Reagan?"

"Yes, she suggested we check out the music store in town. Remember the window display you were admiring last night?"

"Yes, that's right…that's a great idea."

As we pulled down the mile stretch road into town, I took a look around. Today was quite an adventure and a lot of firsts happening. Just the fact that I went out of Christmas Village was a miracle in and of itself. To feel like we stepped back in time and got to reminisce with people who actually had a history with our parents was amazing.

Since today was such a full day and a lot to process, I suggested that tonight we get some rest because tomorrow is looking like another full day. I also have to work but want to be able to go with Declan to the music store. He pulled the truck up to the front of the Lodge but turned it around so that I could just drive straight up the hill. I walked around to the driver's side and he handed the keys over to me.

Wrapping his arms around me he said, "This has been the wildest, craziest day I have ever experienced and I am so grateful that I was able to spend it with you. Thank you for being a part of my developing story." The dropping temperature was nonexistent when he had his arms around me and his lips on mine. The outside world was nonexistent.

He opened my door and said, "You need to go or we are going to have problems."

I am absolutely positive that I would encourage problems, however, I really was exhausted and wanted it to be perfect when it happened, so for now, I said, good night.

Chapter Twelve

Today is December 23. It is also the day that Declan was supposed to be leaving. Thankfully for slow delivery services otherwise he would have been gone like the wind. I feel myself having an Evan Sunday morning, on a Monday, not knowing what his plan is and hesitating to ask for anything or make a suggestion for fear of being shut down for being presumptuous. Maybe after having spent so much time with me yesterday, he will be reluctant to continue this crazy little thing we are having.

Lost in my daydream, while I put my hair up, an incoming text knocked me off my game and my hair fell to my shoulders. Who could that be so early in the morning? Wow, it was a text from Declan. A picture of him lying in bed with his dark hair contrasting up against the crisp white pillow case and his blue eyes bouncing off the screen. "Good morning Beautiful Brie…I slept in a little this morning. Yesterday was great, but exhausting. I wanted to thank you again for yesterday. I know you're working today, and I wanted to see if you might want go with me after work to the music store. We started this journey together, I'd like to finish it with you."

Finish it with me? Is it already nearing the end? I can't believe he remembers I have to work today. I could have told Evan I was going to work while I was making him his coffee and then as I'm walking out the door he would ask me where I was going. Having to juggle all of this parental history in conjunction with being treated properly by a man is a lot to have to manage.

I replied back with a photo of me making a silly face while my hair was crazy and said, "I didn't sleep in and I still can't get my look right. Yesterday was amazing and I would be honored to see this through to the end with you. Will you be in for breakfast?"

Still trying to manage this hair, I threw a hat on and hoped for the best. I'll worry about it when I actually get to work. Two days before Christmas and Christmas Village was bustling. Driving in today seemed to be the better option just in case our sleuthing brought about a tip that would call for us to leave town again. Look at me actually planning to leave town, how grown up of me.

My phone pinged again. "Absolutely I will be in for breakfast. I heard that there is an exceptionally cute waitress that works there with a killer singing voice and a novel just bubbling inside her. How could I pass up an opportunity to see her?"

Nice…he's still interested. As I walked out my front door I kissed my hand and patted my new picture goodbye as I left. By the front door seemed like the most appropriate place to hang my new photo of the three of us.

Some snow had fallen last night, luckily I gave myself a few extra minutes to clear off my truck. When I pulled up I saw that Anna was already here. After our big talk the other night she said she implemented some rules and boundaries. She told Mark that he had to come over early and care for the kids, because she had to get in to work and couldn't be running around like a maniac while he caught a few extra winks. She is also structuring her work schedule so that when she is home, her time with the kids won't be full of stress and trying to get to all of their appointments. The kids have two parents and there is certainly enough responsibility for both. I was so proud of her. This was very different from her personality. She needed to do this so that she didn't give herself a stroke.

Her coming in this early gave us some time now to be together which was so nice. She was never able to take part in the girl talk because she was always getting pulled in different directions. This was also a pretty bold move a few days before Christmas, this is when people are at their most stressed. To be implementing new lifestyle guidelines was savage. She is my new hero. I told her all about our day yesterday and going out of town.

"You left Christmas Village? Like, literally drove past the county line?"

"Well, he drove, but I was in the car, so yes, I guess that counts as going past the county line."

"Look at us evolving into independent women of the world. Who is better than us?"

The door flew open and with her arms up in the air, Reagan said, "It's a new day!"

I looked at Anna and said, "Apparently she is."

"What's going on Reagan, why are you here this early?"

"I broke up with Matt."

"What?!"

"You know, after the show when we were all sitting around talking I realized something. I was complacent. For all the times I have said it to Brie, I was the one that was complacent. He is a great guy, but I can't sit around in what feels like presidential terms waiting for him to make a decision. Even presidential terms have limits. I reached mine. I don't want to be the man all the time. I have no desire to make every decision for both of us and then be responsible for every bad decision that is made especially when I am the only one making any. I want to be wined and dined, I want to be surprised. I don't want to be in charge all the time."

"Well, look at us! You are a single woman, Anna just laid down ground rules, and I have opened my heart and left the county. Let me get us some juice and we will toast. Wait, who gets Matt in the breakup? Anna already has four kids, and I'm not currently in the market."

"Very funny, go get the juice and let's make this happen."

I poured the orange juice and we toasted to strong women, and even stronger friends. I told Reagan unless she planned on helping us set up, she was going to have to excuse me because I want to stay on top of this day so that I don't miss the music store.

"Isn't that crazy, Anna? Did Brie tell you that they are close to finding Declan's father?"

"It's amazing. I'm so glad we all came back here after the concert. I was serious when I said I wanted to do it again."

"Okay, so let's make a plan. How about between Christmas and New Year's? Is that good, Brie?"

"Reagan, you're killing me. I have to get done here."

"Your boss is literally sitting right here doing nothing and drinking orange juice."

"Yes, I see that. How about we all do this again at my house on Christmas Eve? I would love to host that."

"What about Declan, will he still be here?"

"Yeah, I don't know. I'll ask him today what his plans are. Okay, seriously, you two can chat but I'm headed to the back to get some work done. My house, Christmas Eve dinner."

I had put a reserved tag on Declan's table just to make sure I didn't miss out on him. Yes, it was purely selfish on my part and his having a table to sit at was secondary to my need to see him. I also threw one on Ben's table out of respect.

The café was packed as I had anticipated. Everyone was out getting last minute gifts. School is closed today to start the holiday early so literally everyone is out and about. One thing I need to work on is my, I guess, obsession. I hate to use that word because it makes me seem unstable but I can't help looking out the window constantly to see if he is here yet. I'm like a child at the door waiting for the ice cream man.

And as soon as I thought that, the ice cream man showed up. Today was the first time he walked in and walked right over to me to give me a kiss hello. His mouth is always so minty fresh and he always looks so clean and put together. He had his computer with him, as I had suspected he would after yesterday, and he set up his work space. I had almost forgotten, I went to the back and grabbed his scarf off of my jacket. Walking up behind him I wrapped it around his neck and kissed him on the cheek.

"I had this on all day yesterday, it had become a part of me."

With a sexy smile he said, "Lucky scarf."

Now is when I want to die. My face was burning and he thought it was funny.

"Like you said yesterday, I better leave or we are going to have a problem."

"Is that a promise?"

I grinned and walked behind the counter. The morning went by fairly quickly. Around 11:00 am I saw Mrs. Eagan come in. She is not a regular, she might come in on occasion to pick food up to take home. She looked like she was looking for someone and she looked like she was a little dressed up.

"Hi Mrs. Eagan, can I help you? I didn't notice a to-go order, did I miss it?"

"Oh, no sweetie. Is Ben here today? I just wanted to thank him for fixing my water heater the other day."

Oh, I see what's happening here.

"He's not here yet but would you like to sit at the counter and have a cup of coffee while you wait?"

"Oh, it's not that important. I'll see him another day."

"You know what, I would love for you to give me your opinion on the muffins Anna just made today. You would really be helping us out. I am biased so I really need your opinion. Look, there is a free spot at the counter."

"Okay, maybe I can stay for a moment."

I brought her right over to the counter and set her up with a pumpkin muffin and a cup of coffee. I put the cream and sugar down in front of her and watched her put a little bit of cream and half a packet of sugar. My heart melted. I assured her I would be back in a few after I checked on my customers but not to leave until she gave me the review. I ran over to Ben's table and took the reserved tag off and threw it in the plant right next to the table. It only took about two minutes before someone sat at the table leaving only counter space available.

"How is that muffin, Mrs. Eagan?"

"Oh my word, it's delicious."

She was so sweet. I realized I was in the company of many people who are evolving. I'd like to imagine that this was somewhat a big deal for her. She mustered the courage to put herself out there and that is fabulous. She has been a widow for many years now and it's sad to think that she comes in here to pick her food up and goes home to eat alone. No one should have to eat alone. I looked over her shoulder and saw Ben walk in the door. He patted Declan on the shoulder as he headed towards his table and said, "You're still here? Good for you, young man." Ben stopped dead in his tracks as he looked at his table that was otherwise occupied.

"Hey Ben…over here… I saved you a spot."

"This is the spot you saved me? You're fired."

"Ben, what was I supposed to do, she has kids with her. You know she won't have a peaceful meal with two kids spinning on stools. Look, this is a perfect spot, now I can get you your coffee faster," and I gave Mrs. Eagan a wink. She gave me a bashful smile. I hope Ben didn't mess this up by being his gruff, normal self.

I love Ben, but he is so caught up in his own misery he is oblivious to things around him. He can fix anything, except himself. I would keep my ears peeled anytime I walked passed Ben to make sure he was being present. He is a creature of habit and I know just sitting at the counter has probably thrown off his mojo, but he needs to get it together. I heard Mrs. Eagan offer Ben her sugar since she only used half. Ben looked intrigued and thanked her. She told him how more than that is too sweet and she doesn't even stir it. Ben cracked a bit of a smile when I heard him say, "Me either. That makes it too sweet, too."

My work was done here. Just a little bit of effort, that's all anyone really requires. Sometimes when people are out of touch, you need to lob them a softball. If Mrs. Eagan, who eats at home alone every day and hasn't been on a date in ten years, can put on her holiday sweater, a little bit of lipstick and open herself up for the possibility of love, I think that is amazing. She is taking a risk, and that is the living part of life. She isn't letting her age or circumstances hold her back from companionship. Ben doesn't realize how much effort went into giving him the opportunity to make it look like he thought this up on his own.

Declan was typing away on his computer again. Still no graphs, excel sheets or anything of the sort. Other than giving him fresh tea, I let him be so he could get his work done, whatever it was. Ben and Mrs. Eagan seemed to hit it off. Ben stayed longer than he normally does. Usually he is up and on his way to get to his next job, never giving himself a chance to relax. It's like he can't switch work mode off because then he would actually have to deal with the real world. He would, God forbid, have to get in touch with his emotions and actually live other than just exist. I only ever knew Ben after his wife passed so I can't tell if this was always Ben or if this is Ben after losing his wife.

I was cautiously optimistic when I saw Ben drop money on the counter for both he and Mrs. Eagan and seeing them walk out together was the icing on the pumpkin muffin. They stopped at Declan's table and asked him how his car was. Ben said he was surprised that it has taken so long for that part to come in but with the storms, anything is possible. He wished him luck and then escorted Mrs Eagan outside.

Declan looked over his shoulder at me and mouthed, "Did you see that?" I ran over to his table and pulled up a chair.

"I know! I can't believe it. I hope if he asks her on a date he doesn't go out in his plaid flannel work shirt."

Declan laughed, "Give the guy a break. He made it this far in life, I'm sure he can manage an outfit for a date."

That's true. I took a deep breath and sighed. Let's hope he doesn't forget to be happy and turn her off by being like Eeyore. Who doesn't love Eeyore, but I mean, sometimes you want Tigger.

Declan remained typing until we closed. Since it's two days before Christmas, we are closing at 2:00 p.m. which gives us plenty of time to spend at the music store. While I finished closing up, Declan said he was going to run over to the Lodge to drop off his computer and would meet me back over here so we could walk over. Another ten minutes and I was finished. I went into the bathroom to freshen up and when I came out, Declan was sitting at the counter. He had a small, tasteful, beautiful bouquet of red and white roses.

"Hi, what is this for?"

"I wanted to acknowledge the anniversary of your parents' engagement with the red, and the idea of new beginnings for us with the white."

Never have I ever met anyone so in tune with someone before. His grand gestures are tasteful and genuine and make me feel heard. Without saying a word, I started kissing him. He put the flowers down on the counter and was then able to put his arms around me.

"Thank you. Thank you for being kind, and for caring. Thank you for the flowers."

"Let's head over before this gets out of control."

"Agreed. May I stop at my truck and put the flowers in there first? I want to have them at home so I can look at them."

Without saying a word, he kissed me again and then took the flowers and said, "Is there anything else going to your truck?"

"No, do you have the pictures with you?"

He patted his pocket. Shutting all the lights and taking one last look around, we were good to go. He walked me to my car and I placed the flowers right on the passenger seat. It feels like we are so close to cracking this case for Declan. With concentrating so much on trying to locate his father I wondered if he gave any thought to how he thinks he may feel once he finds him. Thankfully we got clarification from Dawn that he had no knowledge of Declan so at least he shouldn't have suppressed anger towards him because he truly was not responsible for not being aware.

We walked hand in hand down Big Tree Lane and into town. The sidewalks were quite busy today as I had anticipated. Ben's silver Dodge Ram was parked outside the music store so now I was going to get an opportunity to ask him about Mrs. Eagan.

Ben was working on the front door of the store so it was wide open for us to walk in. As I walked in I looked back at Ben and said, "How was your breakfast?" He looked up as he kept working on the door and didn't say a word. "Oh come on Ben, Mrs. Eagan is sweet on you. I hope you didn't make her work for it."

"Young lady…I beg your pardon."

"Ben, all I'm saying is that you both looked really cute and she looked pretty happy having her coffee."

He kept working on the door and then stood up. He swung it back and forth a few times and it shut perfectly. Declan had been browsing while I was trying to press Ben for info. Declan sat at the drum set and started fooling around on it.

"Okay Al, you're all set. That door shouldn't be giving you any more problems. If it does, you just give me a holler and I'll be back down."

Al looked over at Declan and said, "Hey kid, you're not too bad," then he looked at Ben as he was putting his tools away and said, "What do you think?" Ben shook his head in approval and picked up his Milwaukee tote and threw it over his shoulder. "You kids have fun and I'll see you later."

"Benji wait, show these kids how it's done."

"Al, knock it off. I'll see you later."

"C'mon Benji, just a quick riff."

Declan dropped the sticks on the floor and stood up. We both stood there, paralyzed, staring at Ben and couldn't say a word.

"What's wrong with you two, you look like you just saw a ghost."

I took a step closer, "What did he call you?"

Al interjected, "That's my man, Benji."

Ben glared at him, "I said knock it off."

"Oh my gosh. How did we miss this? You were right all along. You have been saying I was trying too hard. The story has been right in front of me the whole time."

"Have you all gone crazy? What is going on?"

Declan walked over to him, and said, "Are you Benji Hoke?"

"Son, that was a long time ago."

I stepped beside Declan not knowing how this revelation was going to hit him. "Do you know Ri?"

Now Ben was the silent one. His eyes got glassy and he almost looked angry. "Boy, I don't know what game you think you're playing but I think it's time you leave."

"Ben, wait…look at him." I grabbed Declan's face and said, "Look in his eyes. Who do you see?"

Poor Ben looked so confused. His face was pensive as he tried to make sense of what we were saying. His brow was furled and he said, "Brie, what are you saying?"

I took Ben's tool bag off his shoulder and pulled a stool up and had him take a seat. I kneeled down next to him and held his hand. "Declan is in town because he has been searching for his father. His investigating has brought him here. Yesterday we drove to Woodstock."

Ben cut me off, "You went to Woodstock? You left Christmas Village?"

"I did. We did. That's how important it was. I learned so much about my parents. It was by chance that he found you."

"What do you mean found me? How do you know Riley?"

Declan stepped in. "Riley is my mother. The last two days have been the most informative for me with regard to her. In my attempt to find my father, I learned a lot about my mother. I have some things that will prove I am who I say I am."

"Who exactly are you saying you are?"

Declan took a deep breath, "I'm your son."

Ben started to cry. "I don't know why you would do this to me. I don't have a son."

"Ben, my mother is Riley, her friends called her Ri, she was a photographer. Her best friend was Dawn. You were the great love of her life."

Declan took his scarf off, "Does this look familiar?"

Ben slowly reached up and took the scarf. He stared at it as if he was watching his memories flash before him. "We would pass it back and forth every time we saw each other. I never saw her again after the last time I put this on her. It was like she just disappeared. I tried to find her but I couldn't."

"We found Dawn and she told us that when my mom got pregnant, you were touring with Electric Blue and you guys were about to hit it big. She said my mom loved you so much and couldn't bear the thought of being without you, but she felt that if you knew that she was pregnant, you would not follow your dream. And she thought you'd grow resentful of her and she would lose you anyway. She let you go on her terms. It was the only way she would have been able to handle the loss of you."

"You're my boy?"

"I'm proud to say, I am."

Ben got hysterical and put his arms out and Declan hugged him and helped him up. Ben just kept saying, "I can't believe this."

Now Al and I were crying too. Al pulled out his phone and took pictures which prompted me to do the same. Ben pulled back and put his hands on his face and said, "Let me take a look at you. Thank God you look like your mother." And then we all laughed. "Oh my gosh, how is your mother?" That question took it back down a notch again.

"Well, she passed away when I was six."

"She passed away?"

"Yes, she was sick. She tried to find you when she found out because she was going to tell you about me, then. The last time Electric Blue played at The Cavern, you weren't there."

"Someone sat in that night for me. I was playing with Dallas Trio that night. I can't believe she is gone. She was the love of my life. I was devastated when I couldn't find her. Where did she go?"

"She moved to Manhattan and never told anyone except Dawn that she was pregnant."

I interjected, "Ben, why did you never tell me that you were in my parents band?"

"Sweetheart, you never wanted to know anything. From the time you were a little girl, you did not want to know a thing. The whole town just brushed everything under the rug, to respect and protect you."

"Why is this the first time I am hearing about you being a musician? I thought you were our handyman."

"When your parents died, so did that part of me. Rick was my best friend, we were supposed to do this together. I had no drive after that and plus, you were here. I couldn't leave you."

"So Ri was right, if you knew about Declan, you would have left the band and not pursued your dream. And then because of me, you didn't do it anyway."

"I have never regretted that decision for one second young lady. We may not spend a lot of one on one time together, but I'm always around. I keep an eye on you all the time. Emma was the perfect guardian for you. There was no doubt in my mind that she could give you everything you needed, even as a single mother. She had that much love to give. I had to hang around though and be available just in case."

I gave Ben a big hug, "I know you do. Ben, your last name is Halk....not Hoke"

"We thought some stage names would be cool. I didn't stray too far from my original."

This was never the ending I would have expected. Now what will happen? These questions being answered now created new questions. Declan, of course, now wanted to sit with Ben and absorb as much as he could to fill in the missing years of his life.

"Ben, I wasn't expecting this to be the outcome, naturally, I'm thrilled. Would you be interested in getting together for dinner tonight? I thought perhaps the three of us could have dinner back at the Lodge. Obviously, I'm going to want to pick your brain."

Since all Ben does is work, I was curious how he was going to handle this invitation. It doesn't matter that it seems obvious that this is a priority, he could still decline, that's who he is. He doesn't emotionally attach himself to anything or anyone. He thinks he doesn't have commitment issues because he works so hard and commits to a job. I have explained to him that it doesn't work that way. He uses that thinking as a safety net to get through each day. Maybe now that some of his lingering questions that he has been living with for so long have been answered, he may actually be able to move on himself. "I would love that."

"Hey, Ben, does that mean I am going to get to see you in something other than your plaid, flannel shirt?"

"Young lady, does that mean you won't be fresh?"

"I'm just saying, I look forward to seeing you tonight," I said with a wicked smile.

"Don't mind her Ben, or is it Benji? I'll keep her in line."

"Oh, so you both think you're cute. This should be interesting. What time did you have in mind because I still have a couple of jobs to take care of."

"BEN! I'm sure they will understand!"

Declan quickly jumped in, "It okay Ben. What, it's about 3:00 now, how is 6:30 tonight at the Snowflake Lodge restaurant?"

"See, the boy understands. That sounds great. I will see you both there."

Chapter Thirteen

This was the most exciting thing I could have imagined happening. To be able to actually have dinner with Declan and bear witness to him learning everything he could about his mom and dad was incredible. Add to that, actually getting first hand information about my parents and their music, was a dream come true I didn't know I'd be able to handle.

Tonight was special. It was the anniversary of my parents' engagement, Declan reuniting with his father, and me finding out my father figure has a closer tie to me than I ever knew. December 23 will forever be one of the most important days of my life. To pay homage to my parents and all things rock and roll, I wore a short black dress, knee high black leather boots, my silver bracelets and my dad's silver cross necklace that he wore the night they got engaged. I straightened my long strawberry blonde hair and put on my Christmas red lipstick. It was crazy to think of all that has happened since December 18 when Declan rolled up to the café with no plan, no hotel room and, I'd imagine, no idea that he and I would be having this dinner in this capacity. If his car had not broken down, he would have been leaving today.

Not wanting to walk too far in heels, I parked in the front of the Lodge. I went to the front desk to find Candace standing there.

"Don't you ever take a day off?"

"The boss never gets a moment to rest. If you don't look like a picture of your mother today. Absolutely stunning."

"Aww, thank you, Candace. I'm having dinner here tonight, oh, and I want to invite you to Christmas Eve dinner tomorrow night at my house."

"I know, your handsome City Boy is already in the restaurant waiting and

I would love to be there. You just tell me what to bring."

I couldn't help but smile when I turned to walk into the restaurant. Tonight was a little different in that Declan didn't reserve the entire place. He was sitting at a square table right in front of the window. He had a bottle of champagne ready and waiting. As soon as he saw me, he stood up.

"You look amazing. I didn't think it was possible, but you are more beautiful than the first day I saw you."

"That isn't hard to do considering I had a table on my head."

He sensually slid my long leather jacket off, visually taking in every inch of me. I was only there about five minutes before Ben came walking over. I didn't recognize him at first. He is about six-foot-two, short grey hair, he had on a white button down shirt, black dress slacks and a matching black jacket. Dare I say, he was sexy!

"Ben, damn! You are one silver fox. Why are you hiding behind flannel?"

Ben looked at Declan and shook his head. "You can't take this one anywhere."

Ben gave me a big hug and kiss and he and Declan embraced. It was so heartwarming to see. We popped the champagne immediately and toasted to family. There really was nothing more to toast tonight. While Ben and Declan were catching up on life, I used this opportunity to observe them and see what characteristics they shared. The obvious thing was their blue eyes. I don't know how that wasn't clue enough when he walked in the door five days ago. Not only do they have a unique, almost ice blue color, the shape is the same. Ben has a couple of more years of experience surrounding his, but they are the same.

I watched as they both used their left hand to raise their glasses to toast. These are the things you notice when you are trying to put puzzle pieces together. I thought inviting them tomorrow night to Christmas Eve would be a perfect setting to tell everyone and to just spend the start of the holidays together. Not knowing what Declan's plan was, considering he was going to leave today, I said, "I would like to invite you guys over to my house tomorrow night for Christmas Eve dinner. I thought it might be a nice time to share the great news with everyone and to start the holidays out together. Although, I don't want to be presumptuous."

Shockingly, Ben was very excited about the idea. He agreed immediately. Declan smiled, squeezed my hand and said, "I'd love to."

A calm swept over me when he said that. I feel like I am still coming off my, I guess, low, of the anticipated rejection of Evan. I realize I need to reprogram myself and not expect the same reaction from everyone just because Evan conditioned me. It's not fair to anyone else to pay for the way Evan acted.

It was not only interesting to see the similarities in the their characteristic,s but also their differences. Declan had his glass of red wine, and we know he likes his tea, and Ben had his beer with a separate glass of ice and a slice of lime, and he is a coffee drinker. I love being an observer in this part of their story and just taking it all in. Ben pushed back in his chair and wiped his mouth, took a sip of his beer and said, "I know I have missed out on everything so you are going to have to fill me in. What do you do?"

I took a sip of my wine and as I was putting my glass down, Declan nervously looked at me out of the corner of his eye and grabbed my hand. He said, "Well, I haven't really gotten into this yet with Brie and didn't expect it to happen this way."

My heart sank. I couldn't even imagine what he was about to say. Immediately a red flag went up because my intuition has been questioning this all along. Even after he told me he was in sales, something didn't sit right.

"Gotten into what with me?"

"I'm an author."

Ben said, "That's amazing."

I pulled my hand away, "Wait, what do you mean you're an author?"

"That's terrific, Brie, just like you."

"What do you mean you're an author? You said you were in sales. Why did you lie to me?"

"I can explain."

"Wait, what have you written? I'm not familiar with an author Declan Hynds."

"I write under a pen name."

I could feel my blood boiling. I can't deal with lying. If he is lying about this, what else is he going to lie about?

"Oh my gosh! What is your pen name?"

He sat there almost paralyzed. Ben was equally silent.

"What. Is. Your. Name?"

"Tyler Baker."

"Oh my gosh, Tyler Baker? Tyler Baker, the New York Times Best Selling author for the last forty weeks, Tyler Baker?"

He turned his head in embarrassment as he wiped his mouth with his napkin and under his breath said, "Um, yeah, that would be the one."

"You spent the last five days with me and you actually met my ex-boyfriend. I opened myself up to you. I tell you about the worst night of my life when my parents were killed, I brought you in to the inner sanctum and you lie to me about something like this? You let me make a fool of myself talking about being an author when you have literally had five, number one books on the New York Times best sellers list and you patronize me by talking to me as if I was an author. Oh my gosh, how could I have been so stupid? Well, I hope you had your laugh. Were you looking to just use me as your muse for your next book?" I stood up, threw my napkin on the table, turned to Ben and said, "I'm so sorry to upset your night."

Declan stood up, "Brie, please, it's not what you think, please let me explain."

"You had five days to explain. I would have thought you, at the very least, would understand the importance of honesty every single moment of every single day. You let five days go by. Not once did you ever consider telling me who you really are? You let me endorse you to Ben. I'm sorry, Ben, you might want to ask him for ID and a blood test."

I grabbed my coat as I ran out of the restaurant, then through the lobby I could hear Candace call out to me. Fumbling around my purse I found my keys and got in my truck as quickly as I could.

As I pulled away, I saw Declan come running out the front door. I pulled around the corner just so I could break down and cry. I can't believe I held it in as long as I had. What did I do? How could I let him not only into my world, now I have let him into Ben's and possibly opened him up to heartache? I should have just stayed in my fantasy world of books and movies and the safety of my little village.

Chapter Fourteen

Christmas Eve…In my safe world, Christmas is my favorite time of the year. I love listening to the music all the time and I love the lights and the trees and the decorations. Christmas Day is usually very anticlimactic and I usually end up crying most of the day. I have built it up to be something so fantastic with my dream man by my side helping me cook, watching movies, cuddling under the Christmas lights and just being together.

To date, I have either spent it alone or Evan was there and it was the same as being alone. He would come over midday and then take off after dinner because he didn't see the need to drag it out. "Why does every holiday have to be a big deal?" That was his mindset.

So, even if I had someone with me, he usually disappointed me anyway. Declan, case in point. This really could have worked out to be what my dream Christmas would have been. Men all just seem to be the same in one way or another. They just seem to have that ability to disappoint in some way.

Clearly I didn't think tonight's dinner through because now I can't just sit and cry, I actually have to entertain a houseful of guests. I can't even share with anyone what happened because no one knows about Ben and Declan. It isn't my story to tell so I have to come up with some excuse as to why things are the way they are.

Reagan came over early to help me cook. When she asked me what we found out at the music store I told her it was a dead end. To compound my lie, I told her that Declan had to leave suddenly last night. The reason for me being sad was that I didn't expect to get as attached as I did and that it was my own fault for getting in too quickly to it.

This entire string of lies also kept the heat off him so that no one thought he was the jerk he really was. No reason to cloud everyone else's idea of him since they all thought he was so great. Seeing Reagan here without Matt was a little strange, but she seemed okay. She actually seemed very upbeat and happy, like she had rid herself of a wet blanket.

My little white cottage really did look very festive. You could see and smell the holiday. As you approached my cottage you could smell the fireplace burning and as soon as you walked through the door you could smell the turkey and feel the warmth when you stepped out of the crisp air. There were plenty of fixings on the card table that was set up for the kids to add to their hot cocoa. There was whipped cream, chocolate syrup, sprinkles, M&M's and marshmallows set up on a holiday tablecloth. For the adults, there was champagne, sparkling cider, wine and, of course, hot cocoa. Cocoa isn't just for kids.

I was sad, but it really is no different from any other holiday. If anything, it really is just a reminder to myself to make sure I am the best me I can be, because, in the end, I'm my own date. I need to keep myself healthy and happy so that I can maintain this relationship with me because I am dependable, and reliable, to myself.

Anna's mini van with its Rudolf nose on the grill came down the driveway around 5:00 p.m. She came in with the kids and a big chocolate cake. She brought a bag of toppings for the kids to decorate the cake with when they get restless. Reagan took the kids in the living room and set them up with some Christmas movies. The kids love her so they were climbing on her to keep her in there.

Anna took that opportunity to tell me that she saw Candace. She said, "Candace was a little upset because she said that you ran out of the restaurant last night. Want to talk about it?"

I kept mashing the potatoes, "Not really."

"Okay, you don't have to. You were there for me and I want to be there for you."

"I'm good, but thank you."

"You can do what you want, but I want to tell you something. Jerry came in today to pick up coffee for his staff at the garage."

"Anna, you own a café, why is that so shocking?"

"Well, he asked about you."

"Why is Jerry asking about me?"

"Well, he wanted to know how it worked out with you and Declan."

I stopped mashing and looked at her. "Why on earth would he ask you that? Why on earth would he think there was something going on?"

"It turns out, Declan's car was ready the day after he met you. He paid Jerry to hold his car there because he said he met someone and needed to stay in town. If he had his car, he had no excuse to stay. He loves you. I see it in his eyes. Brie, you actually drove out of this town because of him. Whatever upset you, I'm sure can be worked out. You better than anyone know how precious time is and how important it is to let people know that they are loved. Don't let another day go by."

"Will you watch the food?"

Smiling, "Of course, get out of here. I'll make something up for Reagan, if she even gets away from the kids before you're back."

I grabbed my purse then ran to the door. Stopping short, I ran back to Anna and gave her a big hug, "I love you. Thank you!"

"Go!"

Jumping in my truck, I headed down Big Tree Lane. I pulled right up in front again just as I had last night. Candace was walking out just as I was about to pull the door opened.

"Hey darlin', what are you doing here? I'm just on my way up to your house."

"I came to see Declan."

Her face dropped. "Sweetie, he checked out last night. I figured you knew that by the way you ran out."

"No...no I hadn't."

"I'm so sorry darlin'."

"It's okay. You head up to the house, I'll be right behind you. Reagan and Anna are holding down the fort."

"Okay, sweetie. Oh, hold on, I wanted to give you this. I was going to wrap it and give it you for Christmas, but I just want you to have it now."

She pulled a key out of her pocket. An "old-fashioned" diamond-like key chain with a key. I looked at it and it said 233 on it. "Candace, why are you giving me Declan's room key?"

Her eyes filled up. "It wasn't just Declan's room key. This was the key to the room your parents stayed in the night they got engaged."

Squeezing the key in my hand while I closed my eyes, I said, "Thank you. Thank you."

I just needed a moment before I went home. Kicking myself again, I sat in my truck in front of the Snowflake Lodge. I managed to destroy the specialness of the Lodge. Why I just couldn't let sleeping dogs, and I do mean dogs, lie. Again, I put myself out there and come down here in some grand gesture just to look the fool again. I should have left well enough alone. There was no reason to have trampled on my parents memory by thinking I could hold a candle to their romance. Their love was sacred and this Lodge should have just been theirs. Wiping my tears away, I took a deep breath, turned my truck on and drove back up Big Tree Lane.

Seeing my driveway filled with cars, made me feel better. I'm so blessed to be surrounded by such wonderful friends that build me up, love me in spite of my flaws and suppress their own pain and need to share their memories about my parents, all in an effort to protect me. They truly are all selfless. It's time I stop being so selfish and let them share their stories and their love for my parents.

Sneaking in the back kitchen door, I took a moment to take in the beauty of my Christmas Eve. Anna was taking the turkey out of the oven, Reagan was popping in a Rudolph DVD, the kids were eating marshmallows and Candace was setting the table. Anna turned when she heard the door. Her smile disappeared when she saw my face.

"What happened?"

"He checked out last night."

"Oh, Brie, I'm so sorry."

She put the turkey on top of the oven to come over and gave me a hug. It felt so good to just let it out. I wasn't going to let this ruin my night. My house was filled with the joy I dream of every year. It's finally happening and I'm not about to let a man ruin my holiday again. All that I need is right here.

"Hey, you guys almost ready to eat?"

Everyone piled into the kitchen to see what they could help carry in. There was a knock at the kitchen door and we all looked at each other.

"Come in."

I looked up and in walked Ben. "I hope we're not too late." Stepping up next to him was Mrs. Eagan.

"Oh my gosh, you're right on time…Merry Christmas." I ran over and gave them each a hug.

"Come in, come in. What can I get you to drink?"

I turned to open the fridge and Ben said, "We'll take two beers, with two glasses of ice and two slices of lime."

Smiling to myself I took the beers out and as I turned back I heard, "And I'd like a glass of red wine."

Oh my gosh…"Declan, what are you doing here?"

"You invited me."

Everyone stood in silence, even the kids, and watched with bated breath.

"But I thought you checked out."

"I did. I checked out and stayed with my dad instead," and he put his arm around Ben. Everyone gasped. "It made sense. The best way to catch up is to spend as much time together as we can, so I checked out and I will be staying with him."

"You are?"

He took a step closer. "I am."

I stepped closer to him and he reached out and took both of my hands. "Brie, I didn't mean to hold the truth back from you. I had every confidence in you that you would write your book and I didn't want you feeling intimidated because there was no reason for you to be. The second day that I saw you in the café when Ben was leaving he told you that you try too hard. After spending time with you, I figured out what he meant. You had your story here the whole time. You just needed a push. Christmas Village is the landscape for your story, look around, look at these amazing people, your story has been here the whole time."

"Did you use me to write your next story?"

He closed his eyes and shook his head, "No, Brie. When I was working every day in the café, you saw me writing my first book as Declan Hynds. It is the story of my journey to find my father. Going forward, I am using my real name, because I am embracing my roots. No more giving credit to a fake person. I wanted to honor my parents with my real name."

"So you weren't just feeling bad for me and taking me to these places just to give me something to write about?"

"Don't doubt your potential, right there you just proved you have a wild imagination."

We laughed and then he put his hands on my cheeks and pulled my mouth to his. With his eyes closed, he whispered, "I stayed because I wanted to be part of your happily ever after."

That was the year I had the first Christmas I had always dreamed of.

The Beginning

About The Author

Jill was born and raised on Staten Island. This is her second published novel, but her first under Scarlett Letters Publishing. Although Malibu, California is her favorite place to visit, her stories inevitably always come back around to New York. When she's not watching Hallmark movies Jill is soaking up inspiration from her sons—Joey and Jack—and her close knit tribe of friends.